OF TALONS AND TEETH

OF TALONS AND TEETH

Niall Griffiths

Published by Repeater Books

An imprint of Watkins Media Ltd

Unit 11 Shepperton House

89-93 Shepperton Road

London

N1 3DF

United Kingdom

www.repeaterbooks.com

A Repeater Books paperback original 2023

1

Distributed in the United States by Random House, Inc., New York.

ISBN: 9781915672131

Ebook ISBN: 9781915672148

Printed and bound in the United Kingdom by TJ Books Limited

Ago and prior to the burning and raking and setting of pitch into trackways and when what trackways there were were traversed only by foot and hoof. At that time. From there to there and far away and at no velocity ever thought in error to break the brain. Right prior to weapons against epidemic and virus yet of a moment when berserkers akin to such things began to sprout and spread in a form recognisable. And also following:

Once there was a liquidity beneath a black and boiling sky threaded with red and jagged shapes and then there was a vast cooling and slow solidification happened and now there is a boy/man or a man/boy picking across a great flank of annealed rock. Scare-bird scrawny he is in the torn and drifting sheets of mist which rise from the cracks and crannies. So many ghosts of the swallowed dead. Clad in rags this man-like-a-boy is and shod in little more than ripped scrims of stuff; the white of an elbow, the gnarled nub of a begrimed toe. Tinied by the barn-big boulders that the amassed grey pressure of the scree has pushed into the gullies and between them he bends and plucks and stands and drops over his shoulder into the sack on his back his findings: fungi, flowers, other growths, even just stones that take his fancy. The occasional bone. The long-fingered hand of him with the nails like pale beetles and the wounds both old and sealed and fresh and runny-red. Dirt making runes of the lines and creases in his knuckles and palms. These are the hands between the sky and earth that once both boiled and that in a million hidden fiddlings and nibbles have funnelled the hills within with empty and echoing webs. These hands that scrape moss off stone with a blade. Bag it. The keening of a bird above and around; big bird that throws a shadow through the mist and hurkles a cruciform-thought across the swoop of stone.

Bwyd. Seren. Bwyd. Seren. Food cast down and teats from the mountain my mountain mother mountain just what is offered and here I am. Not all I need no not all of it but it is here and here I am and accept it all I will.

Vast shadows flow fluid down the slope like ink spilled from the well of a titanic scribe. Twinned megaliths emerge from the mist's fringed billows as if in a motion willed within their antique stonehearts and thin and needy the boy-man stops to saw from them lichen, yellowy scraps like the dead skin from a mending flashburn or like the diluted dribbles that circle the moon. From the deep grass at the roots of those stones poke clustered brown nipples and he squats and plucks and eats. Spits out soil and the stiff worms of hard stalk but mostly swallows, a flop of dotted drool on his chin which he wipes away with the back of a hand. Slime of spittle gritted with dirt and commas of dark mushroom meat. Lids come down across the blue of his eyes.

To suckle like this that is all. Like I once did like we all once did oh mother mountain like the calves and the pigs that the Hibernians do keep. Not enough no but what is offered I will take and here I am now and THERE I want to be and this is why.

Bundles of fleece snagged on thorns and thistles like blown seeds, the clocks of dandelions. Out of which might grow ovines more and many. They gather to their spindly spokes droplets and hold onto them, tiny eggs, and thrash in the lifting wind.

The mountain takes a breath; huffs and exhales pale wraiths from its exits and entrances. Sound from these thresholds — clanks and hammerings and the engulfed calls of men.

Grasp this if you can. Wings over it like the birds with their eggs and chicks and food too in the grass or like the suckling pigs or like the wolves that cling singing on in places that cling to them too like they themselves cling because they will not last forever no. Nor this. Nor it all.

Clots of foul froth clumped to the roots at the stream's banks. Yellow-tinged and flocculent and rancid to the nose. Above these sleeps a baby in a bassinet fashioned from a slat-crate and in the stream stands a woman with skirts bunched up at her thighs, the exposed skin of which is seemingly made of the spume's same matter. This way and that she moves her legs on the burn-bed as if seeking with her feet. Nearby and downstream a small boy fidgets on the length of planking that spans the stream bank-to-bank and which teeters with the restless weight of him yet steady and sure on it is he, confident of foot as if long accustomed to such uncertainty.

The woman calls: - Help me here now Ianto.

- But I look for fish Mam.

- You know there are no fish.

- Frogs then. Things for us to eat Mam.

- Nor are there frogs. Nothing you know can live in this. And buried beneath the silt my fleece is now. Come and help me retrieve.

The boy Ianto takes a stick from the pocket of his smock and drops it into the river upstream and carefully eyes it as it passes the plank below. Turns to watch it emerge on the other side and go away. Carried by the current towards the far sea. He's never seen the sea. Yet he's been told tales.

The woman slips and stumbles and uprights herself and wakes the baby with her yelp.

- Ianto! Look what you've done! Making me raise my voice! Go to your sister. It's hungry she is.

- We're all hungry Mam.

- Attend to the infant I said!

Ianto bounds towards the bank — the energy in him, leporine — and squats and places the tip of the smallest finger on his right hand between the tiny pale lips which latch on fast and suck. Gurgles and murmurs from the turnip face and the hands grasping tight on the larger wrist. Ianto observes for a while and then is startled by a *HA* and turns his head to see his mother bend and reach into the river and drag some dripping bulk out and take it in her arms to the bank held to her breast like a baby and with careful and ginger steps. Sodden heft of the thing pulling a grunt from her as at the bank she lifts and drapes it over a sturdy low limb. Like a sheep hollowed-out it hangs there giving bits of the river back to itself in murky drips.

She blows hair from her face and hooks an oily rope of it behind her ear. From flowing stone to this ear's shiny nubs and the sheen of old dirt in the recess behind the lobe. She watches the water run from the hanging fleece with her bare feet sunk to the ankle in a suck of mud. Almost rapt her face is, age untellable from the shadowed features and dark matts of hair that twist and tuft out from beneath the holed scarf knotted across her head, the colour of a sun seen through the haze of a detonation when the air itself barks behind whiffled dust. A rhythm from upriver draws her notice; a steady clockwork thump. Like marching feet of armed men, a double thud-clank unceasing.

- Will there be sun enough to dry it Mam?

Still the baby sucks.

- There's never enough sun. The woman turns to look at her children and offer them a tiny smile. - We will take it to the forge.

Panting rabbit. Resignation in the filberts of its eyes but the sides are rapidly rising. The flattened ears. A shadow falls and the rabbit kicks and tugs the wire around its neck even tighter still and a long-fingered hand — the split pale nails — reaches down out of the smudged sky and works the rabbit from the snare and snaps it once and lifts it limp and boneless and drops it the same way into the sack.

Man-boy squats toadish on scree and examines the toe-knuckle bared through a rent in his boot. An intruder is in there dark within the skin and a dot of blood. He places a thumb each side of it and squeezes and out comes a small gout of red around a pointed pip of schist. He flicks it away. Licks his thumb then smears the saliva on the tiny wound. From his sack he removes a damp clot of some vegetable and presses it to his toe. Holds it there hard. Somewhere in the fog arises a cronking — a meat-bird. High-place familiar. Passing across to something on big black wings at some mission of its own.

A whoop of flame leaves the earth, white and lightless. Down a leat runs water towards it. One to meet the other and create something vaporous between.

Food. Meat. Both mine and yours cig-bran but not the same to share. Meat of thumper for me and mine or might be mine. Catherine. Catherine and Ianto. There will be meat for you in my sack.

Two men stand inside a temple of sorts yet the rain falls on them still. Patters and smacks on the hat and cassock of one of them and rinses runnels in the dirt of the other's face as they both gaze up at the holed roof above. Greasy grey sky visible between the beams protruding like the ribs of a beast famished to lifelessness and long lost on a peak.

At the central point of four tracks above the ancient furnace at Llechwedd Du and the open peat-cutting and on the southernmost of which the geese are sometimes driven in their cowskin-and-tar booties to sometimes draw and distract the boy-man and his little friend Ianto, here at this juncture hangs encaged a man or what was once a man before he was winched up there throatily, his hands and face blackened with pitch against rot and before the meat-birds took his eyes and lips and all the soft parts of his face. Flesh pulpy and sagging and visible through the rents in his rags and turning in the wind this way and that as if vaning the weather or looking about for something that might explain. Hoyed up there between mud and cloud. Talon above and tooth below. Someone had laddered up to him recently and wedged a cornflower sprig in the lapel of the jacket and that tiny blue bloom startles in its colour the watching boy-man with the sack on his back. Staring up at the empty and un-manned thing. Old sack leaking foul inks and ichors into a clotted puddle at the gibbet's foot a-writhe and silent-screaming with maggots and grubs. The boy-man scans it for booty but sees nothing like that and then looks up again at the triple-holed black mask that once was a known face. And the leathered hands that once stacked tatws and mangels in a mound for sale outside the shebeen.

Hello again Huw Twp. Long long seen you fucker of beasts. What brain in there now and what desires it did form the worst of which could only have been a want for one of Sir Herbert's ewes that could only end in this hanging and crumbling wetness and see the green on the skin like the pondskin that chokes the fish. Each gulp the green green slime. You are all of us you are Huw Twp in this I see your ending. In what wise it will come none of us can know but what you are now is the ore of it all. They dig it up. They dig it out. Of us all.

The boy-man reaches out a hand to touch a foot and push and set the carcasse to swing. Circle. Metal-hinge and wood-bracket creak and squeak in the wind's moan. Swivelling full circle once, a glimpse of the shitten nates caked and drooping then back to face again.

A wheelbarrow they found last week they did Huw Twp. Deep in the winze. All I saw of it was the dust it became when it touched the air above but so old they said it was. The men from far away who built the roads and dug the first mine built by their hands it was and all of wood. In the winze at Dyfngwm this. Fell into dust when it met the air we breathe it did. The Romans as they say. None from down there can last up here long nor the other way.

A meat-bird slices out of a low cloud and flaps blackly a few times and alights on the corpse's shoulder. Boy-man watches it scan the tarred face for a morsel. Finding none it lifts itself away and in that bird and in the squirming worms and even in what Huw once was is seen a shriek of resistance against the blackness that funnels the mountain and that the boy-man sees each night between the stars when he looks up on a bent neck at what he imagines to be the vast and icy wastes between each flicker.

Oh Huw. What passions you had like fire. Herbert must need douse them because his kind always do. Oh Huw. Oh Huw.

He hacks up a clog from his chest and spits it into the boiling puddle to see the maggots flinch.

Patter on the hat and cassock and how the rainwater has carved clean runnels in the other's begrimed face; vermicular channels of pale skin through the dirt. This man licks his lips of the rain as if such water has been wanted for months. With tongue parched in this sodden place. With necks bent back the two men look up at the ripped roof, at the cracked rafters up there, their boots amongst shards of slate that have fallen and smashed on the planks and pews. Four walls around them yet they can still regard the great abstraction of the sky and feel the thick rainwet on their upturned faces.

- No other or outer agency, says the man in hat and cassock.

- I fancy mere rot in the wood of the beams and struts but let that not weaken the magnitude and import of this breach.

Hear me? You are in agreement Lloyd? That we stand, you and I, beneath a gap of great significance?

The other man studies the splinters high above. The timber torn into spikes by its departure from itself and that jaggedness dark with damp and decay.

- I'll take that silence for assent Lloyd. As I must. And as I must conclude that the timber up above was chosen poorly. And cheaply. Wood with the worm in it fit only for the pot-fire and yet utilised it was to shore up this house of God and only a lax or untrained eye would see so. Lax or untrained or idle. This house good for God and need I remind you Sir Herbert himself, Lloyd, Sir Herbert himself. A blessing it is that the storm-winds brought it down in darkness and not on the heads of my flock or brains it is you would be sweeping up amongst this shattered tiling.

Lloyd coughs up a clot, purses to expectorate, sees the preacher's eyes in the shadow of his hat-brim and gulps down instead. Not here, not here. There is an edge in the preacher's voice and a buckled shoe kicks hard at a blade of slate and sends it in a skitter-spin across the floor.

- I am not pleased, Lloyd.

- That I can see, pregethwr.

- Oh can you? Such perspicacity man. Oh for the buzzard's sharp eye you have for with such then I might discern how to mend this breach before Sir Herbert himself makes another visit. To which of your men did you allocate the timbering? The carpentry? To which shite-eyed and gleet-brained cack-hander that you retain so pinchfartingly in your shabby employ did you award this vital task?

Lloyd steps out of the falling column of rain and the preacher follows him with hard eyes sharply locked on. Glittering in the hat-brim's crevice like the raindrops themselves. Viper's oculars in a dream-fever.

- That I cannot say.

- Ballocks. Can't or won't?

- Can't because it was a matter of some months since gone. When my Catherine was heavy with the newest child. Long out of the settlement those men are now. To the port I believe where as you know the demand for their skills is greater than here.

The preacher laughs. - Their names are in a ledger yet. You know that, do you not?

- So I've heard it said.

- Kept under lock in the Big House.

- Oh. You mean *that* manner of ledger.

- *And* the other. He sees all.

- So I've heard *that* said too. Lloyd pulls an unravelling sleeve down across his fist and wipes water from his face to reveal more skin, a swipe of it beneath his eye. - We will need more scaffolding.

- Well I imagine so. Or enlist the birds as roof-workers instead. Or the angels.

- Just strong men will suffice.

- Which this settlement has in painful short supply, does it not? Runts and bentbacks. Do you breathe this air about us like the rest of us Lloyd or suck it in through gills? Indicative this roof is of the point this entire enterprise has reached; the unsurety. The, the, the decay setting in. I see it in the souls roundabout as well as in the beams. The souls weak and wizened that sit themselves emptily on these bestrewn pews and this is my concern for if the rain hits heads within here as well as without then what hope is there? The succour and solace held in symbol by this place is gone and we might as well erect a sign welcoming Satan himself. You know the like of Sir Herbert, Lloyd. Vengeful and premeditative both. Flood this place he will if he so much as has an inkling in his nostril of this rot roundabout. The whims of him. And if I can see the apparency of rot then be sure of it so can he.

Lloyd coughs and gulps back again. - There are some yet.

- Some what?

- Good and strong men.

The preacher sighs. - For a life of more ease I will take your word for that. Against the evidence of my own eyes I will take your word for that. And the wood?

- Oak. The best. Some trees were brought down in the storm on Craig-y-Tarw and they await the saw. Fine and fit for planks and props. Send a team up there today I will. Have you a thought to the metalwork?

- The metalwork?

- The pins and the hinges. The nails. Rot in the wood you seek but no rust in the metal.

The pregethwr points a finger. - Because Sion y Gof would not pass off substandard implements. High is the boy's reputation and as I recall I expected his work myself and besides it keeps the walls of the manse affixed to the roof of the manse and sturdy around my family and I. Dare not to blame the boy.

- But the pren?

- What, man?

- You did not see fit to cast an eye over the timber?

- No and why? Because I trusted it on *your* guarantee, Lloyd. *Your* imprimatur. Although how misguided and foolish I was in doing so I am now coming to a realisation concerning. Is this you seeking to defer responsibility?

- I would consider all possible causes pregethwr and only

that. He drinks, does Sion y Gof And eats frequently of the fungus.

The preacher raises an arm to point and in doing that his cape flares like a mantling wing. - You can see the moribund wood man with the very eyes in your head. Look at it. The discolouration. You can see it clearly. In this place you would lie? In *this* place?

- I do not lie. Only—

- Then wriggle like a maggot out of culpability. Accept your portion of blame and make good this your mess. Mend it. I see over all, Lloyd, the physical and the spiritual of this our settlement home and what I see now without any doubt is that in both those capacities you are beginning to fall far short. The wing in a sweeping gesture takes in the surrounding debris. - Get it cleared up and repaired in such a way that this will never re-occur and get it done quickly. Not only is Sir Herbert's visit impending but neither birth nor death nor for that matter marriage will cease due to shoddiness and incompetence and a stage for their holy enactments is imperative. The indignity of rain and exposure on the mourning weeds, is that what you would have? And nor will God's voice be stoppered. This is your mess and your responsibility and this is a Christian community and to worship His name free from the risk of a stoven skull is not too much to ask. Get to it.

The preacher whirls and leaves the chapel on the boom-click of his shoes and in the dark flounce of his cassock. Lloyd watches him go and coughs again and this time he spits, a greasy-grey lung mollusc in the direction of the preacher's exit. A jelly blasted out of a chest-driven *thwoo*.

- Wizened souls, you say. Fucking whoremonger, you. Forever in the puteindy. Licker of cunt and I'll wager sucker of the dollymop's prick. Fall to your knees you do to slurp in such a fever as you beseech your God. Wizened souls. You worship slut and slammerkin and a cur for the trubs you are. That is you. Lap at your own ballock-stones if you could like a dog and I fancy you've fucking tried. *Preacher.* Well this wizened soul puts sputum on yours as barren as the patch of ground your fucking idol Herbert expects me to magick food from. Shite on your shadow I will, pregethwr. And Sion y Gof and Llewellyn. Where are the pair. Useless cunts both.

He hawks and spits again then bends to pluck something from the littered floor — a metal spike. He scrapes at it with a thumbnail. There is no flaking. He throws it away from himself and watches it arc silver through the column of falling water.

Away from the lake's reedy and jaundiced banks the hill flank sheers to the valley floor and across a great gulf of air rises the matching flank cloud-grey and strewn between them like murrain and so very far below is the settlement. Forever in shadow; the crepuscularity here in elemental capture traps all things always between shade and light. Could be dawn or could be dusk below and within this firmament of dust. And too there is the drifting moorgrime and the gases belched from the mine's fires upwind and from the old fetid pockets of such disturbed from the mountain's ruptured bowels. Small houses clump haphazard between the great risings of rock and some grope up the hillside opposite, pinched dwellings once perhaps white-limed but now the general ambient hue of grey becoming brown. The dull nickel ribbon of the river worming through the settlement around and through the mine workings off to the south and half-encircling the holed chapel asquat down there like a brained toad in a puddle. The water-wheel slowly turning. Chimneys thinly lifted which recall to the man-boy the fungus he has recently ingested and which has put in him now a faint buzzing in the skin and an aptitude in the senses of the head to hone colour and sound as they hover in the air closely anterior to nostril and eye. Ant-dots of people and beasts and carts at this remove and the entrances and exits to and from the pits and tunnels that warren the hills resembling nail-holes from here. Miniscule splatterings of pitch. And the graveyard monuments on the opposite flank, the crosses of wood and slabs of stone and crude cairns. All made miniature by height and all so touched with an insect affinity; the nodules of a spider's joints, the eyes of frog-hoppers. Boy-man squints and discerns the gap in the chapel's roof; keyhole rent across which beams hang brokenly like stoven ribs.

Never need such for wedlock. Never approval such as this. Just wolf and bird to allow and bless and no one should need other.

There is high squealing. The man-boy looks up. Flinches as the bird's shadow is cast abruptly across him. Hangs his lower lip loosely as he observes that shadow skate down the flank towards the settlement as if in deliberate aim. Death-angel. Pinioned avenger. Shadow-crucifix targeting the hovels and the holed chapel, to mend or bemoan ask the mountain itself.

And then there is another shape here, sudden, behind the boy-man as if sprung from the stone or the slippery stuff of the air or the leaden lake. A form humanoid but draped in shapeless rags bedecked with leaves and twigs and grasses and bones and with a head halo'd by limp rushes and masked in these things too. What skin can be seen mud-dulled and grimed but with a suggestion of eye-white and amongst the unruled beard braided with browned and wilted blooms, tooth. This figure drops nimbly into a hunch. Unlikely agility next

to the boy-man who impassively regards. The shape speaks
a name:

- Sion y Gof.

- Edric.

- You have a boon for me, Sion?

The boy-man clutches his sack tighter to his chest. - For you?

- Who else? From the mountain yes as you so often do.

Sion rummages in his sack and withdraws brown fungus.
- Only this today Edric Gwyllt. Gaunt pickings of lately days
there have been.

The wild man examines the mushrooms closely, a jeweller
with a diamond, dangled before his eyes between thumb and
forefinger. He places it in his beard and that beard ripples then
the lump in his neck bobs. - And drink you are never without.

- Today I am. You must find a stream. Or is the lake.

- Water? Oh Sion fuck water at this time. There is no
transport in it and this you know as well as I. A taste for the
other stuff we both possess. Across water however I know full
well such transport as that but in it there is only what the body
requires and nothing more than that. Fuck water. I have drunk
sufficient of it today from the lake and the poisons in it too.

Sion says nothing. The wind slaps his collar against his neck.

- Hidden acids Sion. Burn the inwards they do. Turn them
outwards indeed. So thick this morning the lake with dead fish
was I could have walked from bank to bank with unwetted feet.

Sion says nothing. Slap slap.

- Sir Herbert up here of late he was. Saw him I did. Hidden
in the rushes like the Afanc I was looking for eggs. Him and his
man Beynon both together. Attracted both to the banks. Saw
them drawing figures on slates I did unbeknownst. Too far to
cipher yet I heard them speak of explosives. Were I to be asked
my thoughts I might say he dreams of drowning the valley.

Sion says nothing. He and Edric look across the sea of air that hangs all smeared beneath their feet. Edric picks up a stone and studies it then licks it then tosses it away and it clicks and ticks as it bounces down the scree. Faded, the wind. Still Sion does not speak but it is as if the proximate physicality of him alone is enough to draw forth from Edric even only half-human as he appears to be some speech:

- Four days I have been atop this peak Sion y Gof. Four fucking days. To listen continuous yet it is only in sleep that I am addressed and that my ears are wide to hear.

Sion says nothing.

- And what did I hear Sion y Gof. To what words was I privy above the wolves' and wind's wailings, that's what you're thinking now. Is it not.

He taps Sion's skull at the temple with a rigid finger. Sion shakes his head as if to rid himself of a bothersome gnat. Edric coughs and spits.

- Listen to me now Sion bach. What it said to me was that it cannot take much more. Too holed now is what it said the mountain. This one we sit on. More air than earth now I heard it speak in the voice of a banished hag.

Edric pats the earth at his side. Pats the entire mountain as if it is a loyal and trusted hound to him even huge as it is.

- It is more nothing than something now. More air than earth were the words-in-dream. Under the moon I heard it creak and groan and complain as it reaches to itself for a re-join across the gaps and breaches we have made in it and in this way it weakens itself yet further. Like when you sit on a hill of emmetts and it seems a sturdy rest but falls to powder at the first touch of your arse.

- Like the wheelbarrow, says Sion.

- Ah, the one up from Dyfngwm? That went like a spore-ball in rain when it met the air? Yes, Sion. Like that. Pewf.

There is a thudding from below. From within the mountain like a heart in fear restless, rhythmic.

- More explosives Sion. And they drill. More nothingness they create. I know this noise and I know that it is the speech of a turning wheel and not only that no but too of the mountain as an engine, an engine entire. Itself a mechanism to be mastered. And the song of the men's boots as they enter and exit the holes and also and this is important Sion, the dullness and trudge of Sir Herbert's heart and others like his who do not find the ore, who do not mine the ore, who do not extract or raddle or crush or treat the ore yet by some strange and savage alchemy own all the fucking ore in these fucking hills. Every crumb and flake. Oh such men are miners too yet it is in the breasts of other men that they blast and hack and hew. Hear the moans in the darkness Sion. And these extractions both types the same do not improve the land but ravage the land. And both are exhausted. And both will break and soon. This I have been told and to it I have hearkened. A badness is approaching Sion y Gof, the likeness of which I fear we have never witnessed prior. Sir Herbert and his man Beynon at the lip of the lake above it all like God before the flood. Saw them I did. Heard them I did. That man is intent on something he is and that something will benefit only him and his and no-one other. Listen to me now Sion. Warn and start to build your boats because this world does boil with a thousand kinds of diseased cunt.

There is a blood-red berry in Edric's beard. One single released bead. Sion reaches and plucks it.

- Rowan, Sion. For the protection I wear it and nothing else. Use it for that sole and yourself for Christ it is needed now.

Sion studies the berry.

- Do not eat for it puts a badness in the belly. Turns the shit to leat run-off. Like flame become liquid and reeking. It can purge at times but it can destroy too. Hang it above the doorframe of your forge and allow it to remain there. Only that, Sion.

Sion stows the berry in his sack then re-loops the sack around his neck and stands. Coughs and spits. Edric remains seated and gazing upwards. The sack's strap noosing the boy-man's neck.

- Still I have messages more Sion. I have words more to deliver from the mountain's throat. Stay a while.

Sion points. - I must go down.

A squealing escapes the low cloud, high and isolate and hungry.

Strong those nails that I did hew. Strong to hold. Drive them in hard and proper and you could not pull them out by hand nor storm neither.

At the foot of the slope the rent in the roof of the chapel can be clearly seen. The splintered ends of the busted beams. How the slates surge smooth into the gap as if in arrested flow like a river frozen over rocks in the coldest times, iced into immobility.

Very strong good steel I did use. Hammered and folded and hammered and folded again for the strength in the doing. Only bendable in the vice. Support a mountain they could and even a son of God them nails I made as they say but never the weight of bad bad wood.

Below, Preacher Evans exits the chapel; big bird from a trunk-hole now belly-filled with looted chicks. He steps daintily down into the mud with the toe of a buckled shoe testing the depth and suck of it. Shrugs his cape up on his shoulders like a shell against the drizzle and tugs his hat-brim down snug. Makes a giant snail of himself down there in the grime.

Yet he comes in through the cracks he does. Unbeknownst to most that is but without the cracks to enter by he would be nowhere only and screaming for him louder we would be. Hooo-wit, hooo-wit. Now and how my throat is dry.

The smithy, the vulcan: a crude and simple affair it is and open-range with one side wall-less and ajar to the wet fog of the world and its tumbrils and carts both laden and empty and the men returning from the workings like a file of golem sculpted from mud and dirt or going *to* the workings and not in truth much less besmeared. Through the quag the mules trudge bowed beneath panniers of tools and stone or labouring against laden flatbeds with the patience of a mountain. Dragging the spoked wheels through the sludge so deeply viscid that at times the wheels refuse to turn as stubborn as the beasts which strain to move them are said to be although all know a cane-lash or blade-poke are disproof of that. And the music of all this as heard from the vulcan, the thump-clank thump-clank and the drizzle's hiss and soft patter on the tin roof and the voices of the men muffled in the mist and the occasional double-thud of an explosion in the direction of the mines — buh*buhm*. And here in the workshop is the snap and sizzle of the bloated flames and usually the whack and clang of steel on steel but not now, here in this moment, as Sion y Gof turns a mammal into meat. Watched by an avid Ianto with the eyes big and white in the smudge of his face.

- Like this see. Sion digs his fingers into the deep slices in the fur of the coney's neck. The nails' pale carapaces slurped into the red welts. - Then grab, see? Grab. Tight. And then pull hard.

A grunt. And then a rip and a slobber as pelt parts from muscle. Sion holds the hollow skin aloft.

- Like a glove, says Ianto.

- Like a glove, says Sion. - And fine mittens this will make, maybe.

He plops the skin into a pot of water on the slate before the fire. Ianto sees it and thinks of the fleece his mam drags out of the river and thinks too of hollowed animals, all emptied of what they are, all being and matter and there-ness extracted and just shells of things remaining. People too: upright and deceptive and tap them to hear the echo. A skinny patchy cat has leapt up onto the work-bench and with pond-eyes is regarding the bared and shiny muscles of the skinned rabbit in a purple glisten in the flame's light. Ianto sees those flames caught and miniaturised in the pupils big and black and eager.

- Ah my grymalkin, says Sion. - Pws pws. Wants his dinner does my grymalkin.

Ianto reaches out and knuckles the cat behind an ear. The cat presses his head to the touch but the eyes watch Sion as he slices open the belly of the rabbit and crooks out the entrails with a finger. That same finger flicks a small organ onto the floor and the cat pounces and takes it up in his teeth into a dark corner. Ianto squints but cannot penetrate that pouch of darkness. Just a shape in there there is vaguely feline and crouched. With a cleaver Sion disarticulates the carcasse and divides the chunks into two roughly equal parcels one of which he indicates to Ianto who takes a cloth-wrapped bundle out of the front pocket of his smock and opens it to reveal four brown eggs.

- Boiled now are they? asks Sion and Ianto shakes his head and bundles his share of the meat and bones into the cloth as Sion drops three of the eggs into the pot with the pelt. Cracks the fourth on the rim and sucks the slop straight from the shell. Swallows then coughs then yockers into the fire.

- Piediwch ag anghofio'r gwningen. Parch, bachgen.

- Diolch, coney.

- Not now. When you eat him.

- I watched one come out this morning.

- A rabbit?

- No an egg.

- From a rabbit?

- From a hen!

- Ah.

- Is it a bit like shitting?

- What, laying an egg?

- Yes. It looked like shitting it did. From the chook. The wonder in Ianto's eyes manifested in mirrored flame.

A smut from the fire drifts like some burning insect into Ianto's hair and there starts to smoulder. The stink. Sion wipes his hand through the blood-slick on his bench then closes his fist around the tiny flame to douse it. Withdraws his hand and reveals a minuscule rush-bed of frazzled ends stained red. Ianto shakes his head.

- When you do one next, Sion says, try very very hard and see if you can make an egg come out aye?

- I'd like to make my own egg one day I would.

- Try very very hard then next time.

- Will a little me come out of it? Like it happens with the

chooks? Ianto holds his thumb and forefinger at an inch apart.
- Like a play-pretty? All me but tiny?

Sion looks down at the boy. - Perhaps. And that would be very good.

A small and dirty dog — the twiggish ribs — lies behind a cartwheel propped up against a stone wall. Opens one eye to regard Ianto as the boy squelches by. Wet nose a-twitch at the raw meat smell. The boy stops and squats and the two regard each between the spokes, the radial beams around the bullseye of the central hub. Moss on that hub. Long into desuetude this here wheel. Ianto delves into the pocket of his smock and the little dog raises its head at this movement and Ianto takes out an oozing morsel of meat and tosses it through the spokes. The dog sniffs and then snuffles and gulps. The boy watches and emits a smile.

Sion hammers metal rods into points. The hammer-lift and clang then tap twice and lift and down again clang. White with heat the rods are and sparks spring and float. Lifted with tongs and dipped into a barrel of water. Then the freed rolls of greasy steam. With a forearm Sion removes sweat from his brow and shakes his head and his forelock flicks wetness. A dying hiss from the keg. Sion wipes his face with a stiff and stained rag and drinks deep from a ewer.

A clutch of turds in the grass; behind the shebeen in the ditch between the back wall and the rock-bank a dirty bird has been. Thin steam lifts. Ianto turns to look as he re-ties his breeches. Contained within the coils are half-digested leaves and some softened tiny bones. The boy pokes at his spoor with a twig and rolls the pellets apart, one from the other. Holds his breath against the reek. From his own body, these, from the mines and the pits of the skin-suit of himself and nothing in it but waste. Spoil. He kicks dirt over his leavings as he has seen the cats do theirs.

It is just one room — some tables and chairs all wood and a gimcrack bar built from a beam of slate balanced on two barrels. Bottles behind it on rickety shelving alive with the reflected flames that leap and contort in the soot-furred hearth before which the baby sleeps in a crate-bassinet. Over the flames hangs a crusted pot to boil and it is as this that Catherine crouches to stir something in a pail. Lloyd paces about her.

- My cup overflows as it is. A full plate I have as they say and would that were true, on my fucking table. And now this. There is no one I can rely on here nor man nor woman least of all that Llewellyn. Of less utility than tits on a bull is that man.

Catherine does not look up. Stirs, stirs, circular. - I can talk to Mari.

- To what end?

- To prompt her to talk to Llew.

- And to what fucking end, woman? Repeat myself must I now?

- Mari can convey your message and on your return from Y Plas the chapel roof will be whole again and Preacher Evans will be mollified and all will be well.

- And I'll see a moch over the mynydd, soaring like a hawk. I'll do it myself. Slip your mind it will.

- It will not. Notch my arm I will for the reminder as you

taught me to do. She turns her forearm to Lloyd to reveal the old scars in the skin there. Healed and small and many. A stilled swarm of white ants.

- Or Mari will forget or Llew will forget or he will not forget but simply let it pass, slurry in the skull that he has and with the idle in his belly. Twpsin him will do nothing that does not benefit his own narrow world without the toe of a boot up his fucking arse.

The baby grumbles.

- Keep a temper, husband.

- Keep a temper is it? Keep a fucking temper you say? Men such as Llew respond only to a raised voice and threat of a blow or a blow itself. This I know of old and you tell me to keep a temper? I am to be at Y Plas at sun-up which I will not be unless I began the journey a fucking hour gone and yet there is a roof to be repaired due to the, the slow and slacking mind of one who I trusted as did you too if I recall? Mari knows a fine timberman, that's what you said. Recall? So I gave him the work. He needs the coin is what you said. Trusted him I did. Trusted you. And now I need seek him out to make good the bastard shambles of his doing even as Sir Herbert himself awaits my arrival at Y Plas and you ask that I keep a temper with Llewellyn?

The baby cries.

- Not with Llewellyn, no.

Lloyd ceases his pacing and gazes down at the crown of his spouse's scarfed head. The sickles of hair extruding. His brow shunts forwards and down but then Ianto comes through the door and Lloyd turns to him instead.

- And this had better be you bearing bwyd, boy.

Ianto holds out a stained parcel.

- Cig coney I have. From Sion y Gof.

Lloyd barks a mirthless laugh at the celing. - And there's another one! Fucking Sion y Gof! Shout into his left ear I could and catch the noise louder out of his right. Blow a fart in one and put my nose to the other to catch the stink! Tap the top of his head I could with a −

- Lloyd! Catherine now looks up at her spouse. - Christ you would bore a mule!

The baby cries louder.

- Oh would I? An abrupt cough cripples and smothers any other words. Lloyd's shoulders shake with the rack of it then he expectorates into the fire and there is a hiss. - Ah Christ. Give the meat to your mother boy.

Ianto hands over the parcel. Catherine unfolds it and looks inside. - A mouse, was it? Or are these rabbits shrinking?

- Just make me something to eat for God's sakes, says Lloyd. - I need fuel before I go and I must go now.

Catherine twitches one side of her face at her son; a fold comes over her eye and one corner of her mouth rises towards it. Ianto smiles.

The water-wheel turns and turns and the river churns below it. Chimneys point to and gasp at the sky as if beseeching their parent fires, the watery sun somewhere up there like a far-away beacon of warning circling the earth. Water always runs. Inside the planet by the flutter and sput of candle-light men naked but for loincloths attack wet walls and swing metal at them, some lying on their sides in the stone-dust and shards to scissor picks into the rock. What skin not blackened glows pallid and made monochrome these trolls crawl and crouch and cling, the candle-light touching their features with all the pressure of the wing of a moth. Low carts move, pulled by hidden hands by long rope through the shafts and in higher tunnels they are attached to ponies with bowed heads and the clop of their never-resting hooves backgrounds the voices of the men raised but dampened as is the whack of steel on stone by the solid immensity that surrounds. Deeply gulped; mammals slurped into mountain. Intense humidity liquefies flesh. Eyes and teeth the only flecks of non-black in a face. What happens in the outer world on the mountain's skin has no bearing or influence on or matter to this all-eating blackness beyond the fragile flame of a candle, the shape of one tear-drop.

A rope has been slung anterior to the fire in Sion's smithy and over it hangs the fleece slowly dripping and beginning to crisp at the curl-tips. Steaming as it dries. Beneath it and close to the heat sit Sion and Catherine with a book open on the slates between them. Catherine holds the baby to a breast with the palm of her hand gripping the downy skull and the other hand pointing to a page. The baby sucks and mutters. Drops from the fleece plink then hiss on the hot hearthstones.

- The same letters it is, Sion. As before see.

- I.

- You, yes.

- No, I.

- Yes yes that's what I mean.

- What *you* mean? You not I?

- Yes me. And now the next word for the sense of it.

Sion leans in close to the page. Bends low from the waist as if comprehension is contingent on proximity. His lips move but he says nothing.

- Only two letters it is Sion.

Sion says nothing.

- Guh, says Catherine. - It's a "g".

- Guh.

- And oh.

- Andoh.

- No, just oh.

- Oh.

- Good. Guh, oh.

- Guh, oh.

- Go.

Sion says: - I go.

- Thats it. Catherine gives a grin. - "In summertime I go".

- In summertime I go.

- Very good Sion. In summertime I go and…

- In summertime I go and.

- Yes, and what?

- In summertime I go and what.

- No no. What follows "and"? She prods the page. - There. On the paper. What word follows the "and"?

Sion looks at her. - "What". That's what you said.

-Yes but I was asking you. I was not taking the word from the page. Look now and tell me what word on the page comes after "and"?

Sion frowns. Bites his lip.

Catherine, to prompt: - "In summertime I go and"…?

Sion swigs from the bottle. Sniffs and then looks out at the world. - It will rain again soon I think.

- Iesu Grist, Sion! At Catherine's voice the infant gurgles and shifts and Catherine alters her position to hold the tiny face closer to her breast. - The words, Sion! Look at the words not the weather!

Some small sadness in Sion as he looks down at the page.

- I try but to me they are only marks. They say less to me than paw-prints in the mud or rents in the skin of a tree.

- That I know, Sion y Gof. But there is no call elsewhere for such skills.

- Skills?

- To read the movements of beasts or birds, aye. And water. And sky.

- In all places there is a need for food. People must eat wherever.

- Yes but you are a nail-maker Sion and if you yearn to be more as you say you do then you must learn to cipher. What, you would cross the mountain or even by God the ocean to do what you do here? You reach for more, Sion. That you have told me. Over and over.

Sion drinks. - The Cymraeg only then. That I can cipher.

- You cannot.

- I can.

- You cannot, and would you have the heaviness of the Not around your neck again as you did at the school? Have you forgotten its weight and shame?

- I am not at the school.

- Sir Herbert will not care. The likes of him you know well. From Llanbadarn I heard he used a boy's very head as a Not; drilled the word in above the eyes with an awl. That is what I heard. Deep through the skin and into the bone they told me. Wish that on yourself would you?

Sion frowns again. Inner swirls carve glyphs and sigils in the features of his face more legible to Catherine than the printed words are to Sion. He chews his lip. - Say it for me to hear, then. Just to hear and only to me.

Catherine gives up a sigh and rocks the baby in her arms and tucks her breast back inside her shawl. Speaks softly but with a relish evident on her tongue: - Gair hyfaidd, yr haf. Eiddig, cyswynfab addaf, Ni ddawr oni ddawr haf. Rhoed i'w gyfoed y gaeaf, A rhan serchogian yw'r haf.

Sion smiles. - I hear my mother in that. I need nothing more.

- A mountain more is what you need Sion y Gof. A mountain. You need the talent to cipher and in Saesneg too. Cymraeg is a tongue which stops at the port and should Sir Herbert hear he'll take a blade to a whetstone.

The small smile has evaporated from Sion. Drip drip drip and a hiss. in a slumber the baby mumbles in a tongue long forgotten to Catherine and to Sion.

- Will you say it again?, asks Sion

- Say what again?

- The words. The poem.

- For a fifth time? No. And I must now go.

- Go?

- Guh oh, yes.

- Why?

- Lloyd is for Y Plas and so must eat and plus there is the returning shift. Men with thirst and hunger on them hard. Everywhere the need to eat, Sion, no?

- Then here. Sion digs a coin out of his pocket and proffers it.

- I cannot take payment for what I have failed to do.

- Please take it Catherine.

- When you can read a line I will.

Sion re-pockets the coin. - Then I will bring you what the fleece gives up.

- If anything other than snailshells and twigs.

Catherine leaves. Sion watches her go and when she can be seen no longer he moves over to the side of his shop that stands ajar to the world and he watches the purple glower come down to touch the encircling crests and ridges. Sees the shapes on them, on the scree-slopes and rock-falls, the curves and cross-lines and loops of wall and vegetation and he knows everything signified thereon and the forces and movements that scrawled those shapes and what they will release and concoct and bring into being. Not for the first time he fancies that the world was much bigger in times gone and so to tame it God reached down and clasped and compressed it in a fist and bits of it had come up through the squeezing fingers like when a soft-rotting apple is clutched so by a man. Sion sucks at his bottle and watches the men and carts and beasts pass by and he does this until the nightness has fallen fully and then he moves to his forge and feels the fleece for dryness and takes it down. Looks about him. Sees the open book and shakes the fleece out over its pages then lies supine to examine the ejecta, the silt in tiny bits, the shells into which he squints, the twists and ticks of twig and leaf and the specks of nameless organism. And then amongst it all some glitter — some glitter so so small yet a blare in his eye. Lying there on the words declaimed by Catherine which still ring in Sion's skull yet touch his eye only with confusion like the bestrewing of stone random and unreadable following a detonation.

Oh and here you are small seren mine. What the mountain offers yes. Brings in its water which is like the blood of it and this I can cipher and this I know. Over the water and away away such life and living in these things so tiny. Eggs from which the wolves were born and I and the birds and Ianto and Catherine too. Catherine too.

He takes up the nuggets between the tips of thumb and forefinger and puts them gently on an open palm and rolls them this way and that and feels the fires they carry mighty for their size and from a niche in the stone of a wall he removes a box of lucifers and opens it to reveal a tiny captured galaxy to which he adds his latest stars. Closes the box and slides it back into the wall. Returns to his place at the open side of the smithy to watch and read the world, the bits of it that pass.

Like when the lake's skin ripples with the things that move in it does the skin of me ripple to Catherine. In me she moves. Make the skin of me move you do with the things you put inside me and make swim. And in your voice oh mother-mine I hear and not the mountain-mother but her that one long time gone and then I swallow past a rock in the throat. I swallow.

Muddy runnels from which Catherine yanks roots; carrots, mangels. Gnarled fists. Stacks them in a caked pile and coughs and spits and goes into the house and re-appears with a pail of slops which she empties into a corner. Bones and eggshells and sludge and peelings in a steaming heap. Ianto appears as if from the stone of the wall and starts to rootle through these leavings as his mother puts the vegetables into the newly empty bucket. Somewhere a low bird croaks. Ianto selects two empty halves of an egg and attempts to fit them together, to interlock the jagged edges.

- Peid, Ianto. Sbwriel. Brwnt, bachgern.
- Sorry Mam.

Ianto drops the shells and a scrawny chicken appears to scrat and to pick. Ianto watches as it takes up a shard and shakes it in her beak.

- Only four of them there are now Mam.
- Four of what?
- Chooks. Counted them I did. There was five.
- Buzzard then.
- Was it?
- Or fox.
- No wolf?

- Not here bachgen no. We'll get another chicken. Market coming soon there is.

Up at the grey sky does Ianto gaze. - Chicken dinner for the buzzard. Bird in bird.

His mother knocks two roots together in her hands to dislodge the blueish mud. Carrots pallid yet startling still in their caught colours amongst the earth and stone, the browns and the greys beneath the sky those shades too.

At the back door a dirt-blackened face appears. Swathe of red and wild beard, the bottom twists of it spanning the space between clavicles. A cloth hat with a doused candle glued to its top in its own melted and re-set grease.

- Catherine. There's thirty hungry men coming off shift. Thirst on them all too.

Catherine looks up. - They will wait, Llew.

- They will not wait long.

- I cannot feed them without food. Have you seen Lloyd?

- I have not.

- Seeks you he does. The chapel roof. Displeased he is.

- Well. We all must want for something.

Llew retreats inside. Catherine wipes a hand across her face and streaks mud across her forehead. Looks for Ianto and finds him nearby still gazing up at the colourless sky.

Sion gnaws meat off bones. Small bones which when cleaned he arranges on his workbench upended against each other. Vaguely pyramidal in shape. With great care he places them, props them with delicacy, one to touch the other to keep the structure intact. Wipes his fingers on his smock and appears pleased. Bends to peer through the structure to see beyond and through it the fires of his hearth.

If flame could beat and beat it can. The heat in it. Heart proper now in my grymalkin's belly and the meat too in mine yet here it is also in a kind. Beat on.

Like coffins upright two apertures in the rockface. Each the dimensions of a man and in through the left go the backs of men and out from the right come their faces, filthier than those going in as if in the hill's inwards a strange transformation occurs and its sole function is to dirty and darken men and too to diminish them with a stoop and drag. To begrime and enwretch is what this hill is for. One of the exiting figures small in stature and bandy as an ageing and overworked ass is apprehended by the lurking Lloyd.

- Llewellyn Williams.

- I am not him Lloyd. The short man wipes his face with a sleeve as if to remove a mask, the better to prove himself.

- So you are not, Dic Bach. Where is he?

- How am I to know? Been below I have. As you can see.

- He shifts alongside you does he not?

- No longer. Follows mine his shift does now. Changed a week since. Wait and he will appear.

- I have no time to wait.

- Well. Seems he will escape you then.

Dic Bach re-joins the file of men leaving the hill. Moves away in it from Lloyd who coughs and spits. There is the high keening of tiny biting insects and Lloyd slaps at his neck.

After Sion has replaced the fleece in the river he stands statue-still for a while in the icy run. Knee-deep and bare-legged. Seemingly rooted. Burn and throb his legs do before numbness comes in and then start to burn again when he has left the river and is back on the bank watching the colours move through his skin, the pink and the blue and the white. He knows not why he occupies the river as he does only that he must and that others who have gone before him have done the same and that others to come will.

There is a family outside the shebeen. Man and woman and boy and girl and arranged in the mud on stones and stumps about them are their belongings. Crockery and clothing. Pots. The children sit amongst their toys of dolls and tops and hoops and some miniature lead soldiers, a tiny and static battle occurring in the sludge. Dusty off-shift men gather and feel with their fingers the quality of cloth or tip plates this way and that in a search for chips or cracks. Dic Bach takes up a dolly. The little girl sees this and gasps. Dic offers a coin to the father who nods and accepts it wordlessly. Dic pockets the doll and with its head lolling he enters the shebeen and releases a snatch of a lively come-all-ye from the players inside. The little girl watches him go and weeps. The mother squats and holds her.

- My dolly. My dolly.

- I know, fach. The mother kisses the crown of her daughter's head. - Get you another one we will. Lots more. They have dollies in Canada too. Prettier ones than here even.

- Not like her.

- No but even better. You'll see.

And this is no consolation for the little girl. She weeps as her mother holds her. Lloyd approaches out of the drizzle.

- What bothers the child?

The mother looks up. - Dic Bach has bought her plaything.

- Well. For the best, cariad fach. Welsh play-pretties get the malady mer I have heard. They do not like sea-travel.

The father holds out a sheet folded into a square. Stained and frayed at the edges. - Best cotton here Lloyd. From a place like Egypt I believe. For Catherine perhaps?

Lloyd shakes his head. - Llewellyn Williams. Is he in there?

- He was. Gave me a coin for a horsebrass he did not ten minutes gone.

Lloyd nods. - When do you sail?

- Tomorrow morning. Three bells on the tide.

Lloyd nods again. - Well. Godspeed.

The man nods in return. Lloyd enters the shebeen in a quick burst of fiddle. The little girl continues to sob and the woman continues to hold her and the man stares down at the cloth in his hands. A drizzle comes down.

A lament now drawn from the fiddle. Wordless mourn it is, a keen of leaving, yet deep in the fug the mood is uninfluenced by its dolour. These things:

A man holds a spurred fighting cock under one arm as another man strokes its breast-feathers with an admiring knuckle. One side of this man's face stoven in with the eye there swivelling loosely and the jaw set askew to show side-teeth and tongue. Money is passed from cracked hand to cracked hand and marks are made in tattered ledgers. Candles wedged in crevices and the lanterns that hang from beams cast trickles of light across the cramp and heave within. Polyglot and motley, various tongues striping the air to search for ears amenable. The hands that clutch drinking vessels and the faces that bend to slurp from them are all split and begrimed alike. Thin gruel is lapped from bowls. At a table one filth-caked shape sleeps with chin on hand. A grey dust has claimed hair and beards and eyebrows and garments and coloured them one. Anterior to the hearth a uniformed man consults a large ledger with a man beside him in guardianship with a shotgun in the crook of his arm and broken to reveal the brass butts of cartridges. A space around these men as if they are vectors for disease and to stand too close to them would risk infection. The uniformed man beckons at Dic Bach, draws him across.

- What is it Samuel? The doll's head nodding from Dic's pocket. Spastic homunculus enlisted as mascot.

- You ask me what is it? What do you think it is, Dic Bach? I have a space in my book here alongside your name.

- Do you now.

- Why is it there, Dic Bach?

Dic takes a look. - I see it too. Next week it will not be there still.

- Tis always next week with you. Always next week. Twas next week last week and tell me have you noticed? Have you noticed that of late the shift work has taken on a tendency to evaporate for those names that neighbour a space in my ledger? Have a look.

The armed guardian grunts and Samuel spins the book around so that Dic can read it but Dic looks only at Samuel's face. Still Samuel points: - See there? Your name alongside? Strange coincidence, wouldn't you agree? Certain I am that Sir Herbert would. Know he would I do. Indeed he has remarked on it to me he has. In a personal capacity.

Dic takes a drink from his beaker. - I do have something, Samuel. A plaything for your daughter.

He drops the doll on the table. Samuel regards it then pokes at it with his stylus then sighs and nods at his guard who takes the doll and puts it in a bulging sack which he slides out from underneath the table. This sack writhes, shifts and bulges with the struggles of some living thing within.

- One week more Dic Bach. That only and no more. No more trinkets in lieu. An end to it now from hereon in. He makes a dismissive gesture and Dic Bach is gone. Samuel runs the point of his stylus down his list of names. Stops at one. Looks up. Repeats his beckoning and a man approaches holding out by its ears the corpse of a hare.

The whin turns and turns and horses trudge in a circle to turn the drum never stopping. The grind of wood on stone and the whack of their hooves without cease. Turn and turn and turn. The horses and the drum and what it is attached to inside the earth and the mountain itself on the rock and the blackness without end.

- Frenchman. Frenchman.

Lloyd takes the shoulder of the sleeping man. Shakes it roughly and the man jerks and bellows and opens his eyes stickily to look about him in the shebeen and then settle into focus on Lloyd.

- Frenchman.

- I was aslumber.

- Llewellyn Williams. Where is he? He shifts with you, does he not?

- On occasion.

- Where is he?

- Je ne sais pas.

- In English man.

- I know not where he is. Either beneath the rock or a blanket at a guess.

Lloyd's lips pucker. He turns to a large man at his side who has been watching this exchange with amusement.

- Kernow.

- What is it?

- Llewellyn Williams.

- What of him?

- Oh Christ not you too. Where is he man?

- Je ne sais pas.

- Be fucked, Kernow.

- Try the puteindy is my advice Lloyd. He received coin earlier as did I and I'll gladly wager my own in confidence of its increase that he will by now be up to his ballocks in Morag.

Lloyd leaves the shebeen. Casts a glance at his spouse on his way out but occupied as she is she does not see him. The fiddler has now been joined by a percussionist and there is a martial rhythm to what they now play.

A column of men pass Sion as he makes his way along a deep wheel-rut. Like refugees from war they appear all bedraggled and seemingly in shock with the filth encrusted in the grease on their boots and clogs and holed woollen socks up to the knees of moleskin trousers out at the knees and threadbare. Sacks on their backs and candles waxed to caps or cemented there with hardened clay. Battered evening coats and cravats loose and stained at the neck. Some in top hats. Some swinging lanterns in swaying shears of low and yellow light and there is the clanking of picks and shovels and mattocks and the steady shuffle-tramp of their trudge. A couple of score in number perhaps. Several nod down to Sion in fatigued greeting as they pass.

And it cannot take much more Edric as you said. More air than earth down there now you said it is. To itself it reaches across and so its tunnels grow further. Each to each and more nothingness comes about. Annwn opens it does. Send men down into yet there is no need now because Annwn comes to us. Rises it does. Sends its dogs to seek us up here on the skin.

Sion stops outside the shebeen where the little girl has fallen asleep against her mother and where her brother sits against the outer wall of the inn with his back against the stone and his head at rest on his drawn-up knees. The father stands next to the only item left to sell which is a piece of rusting metal. Gangle-pin or hinge. Purpose lost to oxidisation.

- This is farewell then Sion y Gof. We are for Canada at last.

Sion holds out a fist and unfurls it to reveal a scut. - This is for you.

- A going-token?

- For the luck it holds.

- It will be needed. Thank you, Sion. Diolch.

The man takes the charm and Sion dips his head at him then enters the inn. Another burst of sound. The man closely regards the scut, the blob of soft brown fur blood-scabbed at the root. Kernow exits the tavern and sees.

- Amulet is it.

The man nods. - Charm of safety for the journeying it is. From Sion y Gof.

- Give it to me. Tis down pwll isaf in the morn I will be so needed it is. Been issuing a warning that hole has but Samuel will not heed because when did he ever. Will never fucking listen to what the hills say. Nor to me neither.

Kernow coughs and spits and the man ponders.

- I fear that I'll be in need of such a thing soon boyo. Give it to me.

The man ponders further. - A farthing.

- A farthing?

- You need the fortune and I need the coin. To Canada I am.

The exchange is made and Kernow moves away into the smirr holding the scut up before his eyes. The man's wife regards her husband with an expression as hard as the galena that holds the ore.

- Every farthing. Grab grab.

- Coin buys the fortune.

- Does it. The woman coughs and spits. - Does it.

She buries her face in the sleeping daughter's hair. Her husband looks down at her with a thing in his face like a plea.

Catherine decants some dark spirit into a cup. Tar-like and viscous. She hands it across the plank bar to Sion.

- Empty again the fleece was, says Sion, and drinks.

- Again.

- Returned it to the river I have.

- An endeavour without fruit or purpose I am beginning to think it is. It is productive over at Dylife they tell me but here? Silt and grit and not much more. There is no gold here nor anything other precious.

Sion is nudged by a reeling mud-caked man and he covers his beaker with a hand against spillage. Hard to hear now are the fiddle and the drum over the bar's ruckus. The wood-ash in the ale has not yet made the men drowsy.

- Some shells.

- What?

- Snails in their shells, says Sion. - Some of them come out of it. The fleece. Little snails in their shells and pretty they are.

A smile skips about Catherine's face beneath the grime.

- More value in them than in whatever else that river gives up no? You reckon they might take pretty little snails in payment for steerage?

A loud voice roars for cwrw and Catherine moves away to attend. Sion drinks and his eye is drawn to a curling page tacked to an upright beam at his side with a simple line-drawing of a galleon on it and some words, one of which he recognises:

- Guh. Oh. Go.

Sion empties his cup. *GO.*

Rackety door with vertical slits unflush, the gaps between which allow cold air in and watery firelight out. Cracks of it in the vertical; slashes of diluted yellow. It shudders with the rap of a fist and is opened. There is Lloyd at the threshold.

- Mari.

- Not in tonight Lloyd she isn't.

- Who?

- Morag. Abed she is with her monthlies. They cramp her terrible.

- I seek not her tonight.

Mari steps aside to admit him. Little more than a one-room shack is the puteindy. Some sticks smouldering in a grate and some shabby chairs and a sheet tacked up across roof-beams to create a triangular chamber across which shapes move as if in a shadow-play, limbs now shifting and now interlocked. Lloyd looks about him and spies a young woman as stiff-backed as the chair she's on with her hands clasped in her lap and some browning and drooping blooms twisted in her hair.

- New cunny, you?

- She cannot speak, Lloyd Mari says. - Nana is her name. Nana the Noise we call her.

- And her muteness is the result of what?

- Arrived yesterday she did from Hereford way. Fled a cowman there who took umbrage at the little giggle she gave when she saw the pignut he was sporting so proud. Him thrusting it out so.

- And the shock of it struck her silent?

- No, Lloyd, he'd been at the gelding that day so he had his blade and the pruning-mood on him both. Took her tongue he did. Struck her silent indeed.

- And she told you this tale how, woman?

- She can write for God's sake. Of course she can write. And in this place she will find safety will she not?

Lloyd turns to Nana. - Make a sound, girl. Utter a word.

- She has no tongue Lloyd.

- Speak to me I said.

The girl moves to stand behind the chair to make a flimsy barricade between her and the man. She makes a wordless whisper and a shape comes out of the dark recess between the dresser and the wall and drifts to her and holds her and turns to put a glower on Lloyd from flinty eyes in blueish smudges and berry-red lips in uneven stubble.

- You would do well to be as quiet as her you would, Lloyd says, this shade out of the powdered and coloured face. - Afraid she is. And work she will not until she is not afraid and that time will not come unless and until men like you learn to hold what she has had in rupture taken from her.

Lloyd sneers. - Mollieboy. And to what employment do you put *your* tongue, you unnatural? What offence to God and nature do you nightly perform foul and freakish and abhorrent to the acceptable manner? Upbraid me never, mollieboy. Insect sodomitical.

- Tell me why you're here Lloyd and then be on your fucking way. Mari sites herself before Lloyd. Arms folded across her chest below the decolletage. A head lower than Lloyd, her brow at his chin. - If you are here only to berate and pour scorn and affright then leave now. And do not attempt to tell me you have never used any of my women in that way even when they were as clear as the river once was that-

- Ah, fucking whisht woman would you ever. Believe a whore's demands and be made a fool and bankrupt both. Hold that fucking tongue.

The mollie takes Nana over to his cwtch behind the press; a niche containing a coiled blanket and a chamber-pot and a half-eaten bowl of slop. Some cosmetics on a slab of slate. Lloyd's sneer is disrupted as he hawks and spits and then nods at the shadowed sheet behind which the sounds have now become yelpy in urgency.

- Behind there. Who?

- Not Morag. Told you I have.

- Not the cunt. The man with it.

Two strides take Lloyd around Mari and he tears the sheet down and there's a salt-white arse bepimpled and pumping between spread legs. The red blaze of Llew's face looks back over a shoulder. Lloyd grabs a fistful of shirt and yanks Llew out and up.

- What in the name of Christ Lloyd!

Llew tugs up his breeches and fumbles at the fastenings and the girl beneath him covers herself with a shawl. Mari roars to take it outside whatever it is but Lloyd ignores her.

- In fuck sake Lloyd! What a time to interrupt a man! Could it not fucking wait?

- Timber, Llewellyn.

- Timber is it? Llew tucks his shirt into his waistband. - You break the satisfaction of my need to enquire of fucking timber? Sure I had a sturdy piece of it on me barely a minute ago did I fucking not?

- A big hole in the chapel roof there is. This may have come to your notice.

- And what of it?

- A collapse. During the night hours so skulls were spared with mercy but rot in the timber is to blame. Rot in the timber.

- Ah.

- 'Ah'. That's the extent of your remarks, is it? "Ah", you fucking —

- Take it outside, Lloyd!

- Stay quiet Mari lest I make you a silent twin to your new whore. An "ah" will not appease Preacher Evans Llewellyn nor Sir Herbert himself and nor will it restore my reputation. Clearly I recollect your claim that you were possessed of good wood. To be trusted you said.

Llew stays silent.

- What you did with that trustworthy wood I neither know nor care but what I do know is that the wood you used was sub-fucking-standard and I also know that if the chapel roof is not in repair when I return from Y Plas then you will stumble one night into a pit-shaft. Worse, even, I will drag you tethered to Y Plas and hand you over to Sir Herbert's men. From hereafter that roof hangs over your head only and your mortal interest is in securing its maintenance. Hear me, you fucker of pigs, you?

Llew's mouth flops open to speak and Lloyd grabs his face in one large hand and lifts and hurls it and the body it is attached to in the direction of the door. A scattering of chairs and a jumble of limbs. Llew scrabbles half-standing for the door handle and scuttles outside.

- Ych y fi, Lloyd! Mari is re-pinning a corner of the sheet to a beam. The girl has buried herself deeper in the shawl. Just a hair tussock to be seen. - He has not paid!

- He has not paid?

- No! Deprive a worker of her earnings would you? Christ man!

A voice comes from beneath the shawl. - I do not offer it for free!

Lloyd shakes his head. - You let a man spend prior to exacting payment? Cunt before coin? Good God. He moves to the door and looks about him. Glares at the mollieboy's face glowering from the corner-shadow and spits. - This place. This place.

Lloyd leaves.

The cart is a crude flat bed of uneven planks pulled by a mule which is steered by a figure cowled up against the drizzle. Facial features completely obscured. Pilot of people this night-headed anonymous tugs back on the reins to halt the mule's bowed trudge outside the shebeen. No words. The woman moves towards the door of the inn but the man stops her with an elbow-grip.

- No, wife. You will not.

- But I must.

- You must not. There will be tears and entreaties and you will find it difficult to bear and no doubt dissuasive. As might I indeed and certainly will the childer. And the tide will not wait besides.

The woman gathers her children to her and they all three clamber up onto the cart. The man hands up three cases and then hoists himself up onto the planks and hisses and examines the wood shard that pierces his palm. The driver holds out a hand, thin and white and twig-fingered out of a drooping sleeve into which the man drops a coin. The hand hides the coin. The reins are flicked and the cart trundles away from the inn rocking across the ruts unheralded in the damp night. A board tacked to the back of it reads:

TJ EDWARDS
CEIRION
BRYNGOLAU
THIS IS HIS CONFEYANS

Into the night the cart creaks. The wheels of it slowly turn. Perhaps there is some small sobbing to be heard behind the light rain's sizzle.

Sion y Gof leaves the shebeen and stands there looking left to right then left again to the west where the sea is said to be. The sea and over it Eire. And beyond that Canada, far away.

Guh oh. Gone then now. More gone away. And soon there will be no more left to go and dead and empty this land then will be. A waste. Only the dogs and the crows that pick. The fur and the feather and the tooth and the talon and the fangs and the claws and the wings. And the mountain will make a happy noise like my grymalkin does when he eats and the wolves they will return. Might the river awaken again. Birds above they know this to be true and that is why they wait and have taken Huw Twp's eyes so that they might see more.

A colossal spinning goes on as it always does towards and away from the moon. Many things sleep in the bare branches and beneath stones and in burrows and the background clank-thump continues even as it accompanies a lesser traffic now and the owls do hunt on silent wings with their faces concave in their contours to suck sound. Smokestack fumes appear as the frailest of webs spun across the moon's pale and lifeless face.

The wall which the headboard abuts is patterned with mildew. Dark shapes slowly growing like countries coming into outline on a cartograph or continents of shadow. Three figures asleep on the bed; Catherine bracketed by her children. The baby a doll on its back spreadeagled and Ianto foetally curled. Three breathings in the chamber's trapped dank. A smear of grey light at the windowpane.

In the wan light returning tumbles a leaf close above Sion's head. There are few trees nearby and those that are stand skeletal and denuded of leaves yet here one is bat-like but slow and rolling crisp and curled end-over-end through the cone of Sion's vision. As if in a flight willed and applied and not merely whimmed by the wind. Sion stands and watches and fancies it a gift from the come-again dawn even as the greasy soot starts to gather once more at his collar and cuffs and eyelids.

I know of this word cariad or love as it is in the Saesneg. Know it in my inwards in the sweet places inside. Have it in me even for this falling leaf. Had I it in me for my mother and she for me it is to be wished. And in me it is for my grymalkin and the birds that are his meat and rodents and even for the coneys that are my food. For the emmetts even and the worms the grubs as they are called. Even them. The chooks. Ianto.

Catherine. At these moments when the light returns that word and what it means comes with the light and this I feel and know.

The ridge of a hill is a smudged swipe of charcoal against the lightening sky. This wide and empty space. Great surge of earth bisected by a beast-track along which Lloyd walks solo. Sack on his back and hat on his head. Wearily whistles a few bars of a tune and then falls silent again. Huffing breath in the cold and oily dawn. The echo of his whistle following him like a memory of something that is yet to happen.

At an entrance to a cave stands Sion. Morsel for a massive maw. Stones about scored with sigils to ward off evil or misfortune. Scattered anti-hexings. He holds a cloth bundle tight to his navel like a timorous offering to the cave itself, the beast of the mountain whose hungry gullet it is. He emits a wordless shout then waits and calls again. The mountain gulps his voice then belches it back to him weakened. The wet walls to be seen. Sion waits more then places the bundle just over the threshold and turns to leave but is then called back by a grunt. Borborygmus from the mountain's tract. A shape leaves the cave's caught blacknesses and takes the form of Edric Gwyllt, stripped somewhat of the recent adornments from the hair-froth of his head and face but the grime still on him and in him like the dark dust from the mines down which he has never toiled. The flash of his eyes and teeth in the murk that surrounds.

- Sion y Gof. Good Christ boy, do you never sleep?
- I bring bwyd Edric.

Edric squats and takes up the bundle. Opens it to reveal

some bones and an egg and a few bright berries. Three mushrooms. He sucks a small bone and gestures with it for Sion to sit. The two of them tiny anterior to the great stone throat behind. Absorb. Absorb.

- And you bring a problem too, Sion? Some sadness or botherment there is on you more than usual and that I can discern.

Sion shakes his head.

- Then what boy? A gift however meagre is never made unconditional even from you. And I see some rain in them your eyes. Smirr in their blueness there is. Sit by here and put the weight in you on the mountain and on me. Or some of it at the least.

Sion settles on his bony arse. Still does not speak. Observes as Edric peels the egg with care and removes the shell in one crazed piece like a snake's sloughed skin. Edric eats the egg in one chew. A distant boom echoes down the valley. Small yellow crumbs of yolk in Edric's beard as he speaks.

- Bolen, hear? And still they blow the bowels from the earth. More space than rock now Sion, more tunnel than mountain you remember what I said. The warnings have been clear for some time but there are no ears that can or will hear. A Spaniard I recall, shat his own guts out over the side of a ship out of India. Four years ago perhaps. Hung from his hole they did Sion. Big bag of his inwards. Blue-ish. And they're doing that to the mountain beneath us. This very mountain our chair. Blasting its guts away and out and like that Spaniard it too will expire screaming and hollow.

- It reaches to itself, says Sion at last.

- What?

- It reaches to itself. Told me that you did.

- I did?

- You did.

- And I was not wrong. Hear it in there I do. Edric points a thumb over his shoulder. - Inside. A groaning as if in a straining to reach. The rock yearns to touch the rock across the emptiness it does. To re-join with itself. How it must yearn with the age of it. Close to itself before the sun was alight it was and how long has it taken to break that? Less than one blink in the entirety of its time Sion. Source and essence of what we are and all the urges for chaos and order both. The damage itself which like its brother pain never ends the fucking world and only death does that and this the mountain knows that until you return to the earth that gave you there is a heap more of it lying in wait. Accept like a fucking man and be sure to return some of it to its origins. Whatever that or they might be. Mostly not what you surmise it's going to be but that you must know by now. Ah Sion y Gof I do not know. Perhaps we are but forms in a dream which the mountain is yet to awake from. Oh I have the schoolmaster mood on me this morn I do.

Edric bites into a berry and a purpleness bursts and smears his lips and in close focus with Sion leaning in like he is Edric is colourful indeed; the maroon of the juice and the tiny crumbs of yellow and the spikes of small green snared in his beard and too the colours of the tangled wires there, brown and tawny and white. Harlequin man from the mountain's gut. - Understand do you?

Sion stays silent.

- Well, something there is that hurts you Sion. Some reaching across some loss, that I see mirrored in you now. Were I to rap a knuckle on your back there would be an echo I know.

Sion takes up two small stones one in each hand and begins

to grind them together. At this action Edric nods as if some inkling has been confirmed.

- Look here at this now Sion. He rolls a tattered sleeve up to his elbow and licks a thumb and with it rubs grot away on a patch of his forearm to reveal beneath it a crude tattoo of a horned head. - See?

Sion nods.

- Head of what they call a bison.

- A what?

- A bison. Big cow similar. Size of a hutment Sion they are.

- Biiiiisssssssoon. Sion whispers the word as if savouring a flavour.

- Found in America they are and seen them I have. Great great numbers across the plains like a meat-sea. Watch the first of them pass and see three moons you will before you see the last yet hear I do that their numbers are lessening because something is coming Sion oh yes. A change in man that has not yet been seen and for which those without it and the world itself are unreadied. Beasts like stars in the sky I did see. Numberless. Run together and the very mountains did tremble as with distemper. The noise of thunder. And the mountains in that place Sion as to shrink ours to an arse-pimple. Oh and lakes like oceans and forests to cross beyond a lifetime. And those beasts those bisons once a thing akin did dwell here too but no longer. Gone from here now they are. Bears too.

- Bears?

- Think brock but horse-size. And mud-coloured. And cats like cows too Sion that hunt and eat the bison so big are they. Eat men too they do. Grymalkin so grown and imagine the claws of him then. Imagine the teeth of him then. And the wolves, Sion! So many wolves! A land of marvels that place is.

This you know and why because been there in your dreams you have and so big is it that the mind of a man could only ever hold a crumb of it yet what is small enough to be cupped in the hands and hearts of men can and will crush it like a snail under your shoe. This is the thing so unknown to the world yet here now it is. So I have been there and so I have returned. Look again Sion.

Edric spits on the webbing of skin between his thumb and forefinger and rubs at it to show more drilled ink; a forktailed bird in flight.

- Seen this mark you have on men come from the port Sion yes? Most who take to the sea and come back again do bear it. Because it means that like these birds you will one day return.

Edric takes a black-crusted pipe from somewhere in his smock and fills it with dry leaves which he pinches out of a skin pouch and strikes a lucifer on the mountain and touches it to the bowl and puffs a ghost of smoke out into the damp air. Sion follows it with his eyes. The drifting wraith of it. A veil between him and the opposite peak.

- Like wants like Sion, see. This is it. And what it needs it will surely find because it sees itself and finds itself in a place where it might not be. Even if invention is what is required. Understand this I know you do or have some small grasp of it just.

He passes the pipe to Sion. Sion smokes and hands it back. Somewhere nearby a small rock slips and bounces down into the mist and a thing mewls unseen somewhere else.

- Ah Sion y Gof I do not know. A schoolmaster's is my mind today yet of what discipline in particular it has no more notion than a dog has of the metalwork you trade. To express is the need and that is all. Like what the hills give up or what they discover in the pits, the remnants of lost lands and those that lived on them. The wheelbarrow. Heads of axes and arrows and the Noah trees off the shores and the artefacts all pretty ornamented for no other reason than that. To please the eye of ye. How can we know the reasons. Enough to know that those things and the stones that stand on all the peaks about were here long before the chapel. Long before each and every one of the fucking saints.

He puffs again at the pipe and re-sends out the smoke-ghosts into the fog that claims them as a parent embraces a child. Sion thinks of that — of things emitting their substance in shreds and sending it all mutable into the world and through the madly differing stuffs of it as if in wild adventure. Holding the knowing that the original matter will be one day returned to preferential or if not that then never to be properly nor for any appreciable length escaped.

- There might mayhap be some means in the port Sion. The restlessness in ye. I have seen it often and once it was in me. Many times it took my sleep and set my blood to run like the river. Set off the bolen in my head it did. Over and over again. Boomboomboom like that unceasing. And there is it seems no pattern to your story that might veer it from mine or if there is I cannot see it and so I will guide you to follow it where it must take you but I will say that you should flee from any grinning gangmaster who promises you passage and employment on a man o' war. Heed that advice if nothing else because believe me it will destroy you. In many several ways Sion. And the hunters that haunt all ports and harbours, them who can smell and are drawn to the lonesomeness and desperation. Such stuff the predators await. As can be seen in the wolves. Them few that remain. D'ye have me here Sion?

Sion nods.

- Ah by chance there are life-lines yet to take you out of this.

Once more I do not know. Less white in my hair there was when in the port I last was. Changes will have occurred I have no doubt. So attend to the little ones Sion for they do not alter and they it is who make and have always made the signs. Even before such beasts as us were here.

- The little ones?

Edric nods. - The little people aye. The cochyn. The pobl fach. This I saw in Eire and in other lands too that when the little ones do go they take a culture with them. With them it does die and the particularity of its hope dies too forever. Survive separately it cannot even so small as they are and when it is gone it is gone and there will be no return. The little ones, I do not hear or see or smell them anymore beyond their wailings in their ailments and who is to say that such emit only from throats of rock not flesh. Are nothing more than sounds bounced back from the stone. Ready yourself to fare-thee-well the little ones Sion and welcome in what the world has never before seen. Never before suspected the depth of it nor the spread of it in its quality of utter unmercy.

Another rumble from along the valley. Faint like thunder over the horizon but within the earth and not the ditchwater sky. More stones shift and tumble. More things in the mist mewl and croak.

The pipe is passed again and Sion smokes. Returns it and Edric points the stem in the direction of the sound. - And with that disturbance goes yet more internments Sion. Burials still more and never to come again. Storms in the stone is what it sounds like yet resist any associations of an otherness to cruelty because that is all we wait on. Storm? We will not see the lights in the sky nor the colourings nor the tall beings made of whiteness that leap the peaks in an instant and before which I have seen you stand agog and in awe Sion.

None of that awaits. What we sit on was once a volcano and I did see one such enraged and wondrous in a land of ice and fire and now what is this our seat? A lump of stone spent and exhausted and all burnt out and nothing more. What approaches this place is a dread the likes of which it has never encountered yet and mark me here it will not feel like dread. It will be a state in which you will speak or dream or feel nothing. Like these hills you will be — more nothing than something. Filled with holes. The only songs those that bounce back from the walls the life of them long gone and no re-birth. Throats clogged with dust which no songs or attendant sweetnesses can slake. At the lake I have seen them and I know what such marks signify even if that has yet to be seen in this place. A dragon's tooth is that man Herbert, sown in a furrow and isolate and nothing but ash will be its spawn. Ash and dust and nothing beside. What wants itself wants itself and find itself it will and nothing will stand in the way of that. Not man. Not mountain. A new kind of power is entering polluted hearts Sion. Think on the little ones and watch for what they tell.

A further plume of fume leaves Edric's beard like exhaust and builds a vaporous barrier between his face and Sion's. Hangs there unbreaking despite the quickening wind.

- Enough I have said now Sion. Bored with my own voice I now am and my throat is clinker-full. Is there a potable with you? Even clean water just would satisfy me now.

Sion shakes his head.

- Well fuck it then, says Edric, removing his mask of smoke.
- Sleep some more I must. Tired I am.

Sunlight, at the last. Here in this walled garden the drizzle has ceased and sunlight bestows favour. All is neat and cultivated within these walls and fruit trees are espaliered against the red bricks with their limbs outspread as if awaiting execution. Small fruits depend. Berry bushes and bee-hum and birdsong. Rills are arrayed in rigid parallels at one of which Lloyd crouches to pull root vegetables from the rich soil. he brushes them free of muck and places them with care in a tub alongside clustered alliums and bunched herbs. The green and scented froth of them. A delicacy to Lloyd's movements there is, a hint of recreational calm as if here in this walled and fecund place is a serenity which infects or demands to be mirrored in those who do not possess it as a token of admission through the gate.

Deep, deep in the mountain some men break through into a stope. The tightness of the tunnel blown silently and abruptly outwards into a chamber so big that the light of the lanterns touches no sides or ceiling. Size of this chamber matched by the magnitude of the hush. The men's faces in lamplight. Both crushed and colossal they are here in this endless vault. Before their faces cave-spiders seek to escape the light and the heat of human breath and scurry spindle-limbed up their silver cables into the black void.

Two women on the riverbank little grown out of girlhood. Booted and be-shawled. Raggy hoods over their heads. One with wild carroty hair tumbling in rolls about her ears removes her boots and puts her pale chilblained feet into the water and instantly snatches them back out hissing through her teeth.

- Like fucking ice it is!

- That I know but the body needs the shock, the other woman says. - Do it together we will.

She too unlaces and tugs off her boots and at the count of three both women plunge their feet into the torrent. Whoop and grimace and bare their teeth and make noises of escaping air.

- Oh God. Oh God. This a body cannot bear.

An accent from the north country. Alba.

The other woman's jaws chatter. Her teeth clackening in her face. - That's kind of the notion Morag. For a body not to bear it.

They sit for a moment unstill with the trembling in their limbs and their chins all a-chunner.

- Are you afraid?

Morag nods.

- Mari and the mollieboy know what to do and the practice in which to do it. The method of it all. This is a thing they've done many times prior.

- With ye?

- Not with me no. Or not yet although I cannot surely avoid the affliction for the indefinite. But many others. Been present as witness I have at some.

- I've heard tales tho Lou.

- Aye and not all offered truly. Of that I can guarantee.

- Not *all?*

Lou shakes her head. - Once there was more to chance than knowledge in these operations. We know more and further now.

- We do?

- Yes, because with each, um, unsuccess we learn more, says Lou. - About the power of various purgatives and the such. Which work and which don't and what the body, the mother's body, can bear. Seen it done I have more times than you can count Morag. Trust to Mari and the moll. Know how to do this they do and bring the necessaries they will. Until they come let your feet go unfeeling to increase the shock in the womb that is necessary and curse the poison that drips from all cocks.

Morag coughs and hawks and spits. The current carries the swirl of mucus away from her. With one hand in a circular motion and with an expression of ponder she rubs her gravid belly.

At the side furthest from the windows in this kitchen large and bright hangs a black sheet anterior to which Lloyd suspends things from hooks. A leek and a cabbage. Observing him is a man at an easel with his hands on his hips. On a long trestle and below the hanging things sit mounds of other vegetables and herbs. Flowers. The man at the easel appears entranced.

- So tell me, he says. - Those you have suspended. Why might that be?

- To arrest the spread of moribundity.

- Oh?

Lloyd nods. His eyes stay fixed on his own hands in their movements careful and measured. - Should one item alone get the blight and it abuts the others then the blight will spread. The dampness in the touching, such state the rot desires and needs. To infect and spread itself. It lives see.

- I understand.

- Hanging some like this will admit the free movement of air and obstruct the reproduction of the animalcules. Dry them out you see.

- I understand. The artist takes up a brush and makes marks on his stretched canvas. Three quick strokes of green. - And earlier this morn there was fungus I saw. What became of it?

- Ate it he did. With eggs and a pig knuckle.

- Who did? Beynon?

Lloyd nods. - Told me he is partial he did.

- A shame. The texture of fungus lends itself to representation with more affinity than anything else I see here. The earth in the gills and such.

Lloyd places the soft alarm of a cabbage with care on the trestle foregrounding it between the artist and the materials for the still-life. The green in the leaves. The rigid ribs.

- To the left, please, a little, Lloyd.

Lloyd obliges.

- And just a little more if you would. That's it. So the light is captured by the, the tubes on the leaves, what might they be termed?

- The veins.

The artist looks over his canvas at Lloyd and grins. - Of course. The veins. What else?

He leans to his easel once more.

- More, Morag.

The mollieboy presses the bottle again to Morag's lips. She slaps it away.

- Dwarny more.

- You must drink it Morag.

Insistent the mollie is as is Mari who holds Morag's head still as the bottle is tipped to her lips. Mari's breast pressed to Morag's back to keep her upright on the brown river's mud-sucking banks. Morag coughs and splutters and some of the spirit slicks with the saliva across her chin.

- Gun sick.

- That's the idea, says Mari. - Let it go my girl. Let it all go.

An abrupt blurt of vomit leaps down the front of Morag's smock. Lou leaps up from her nearby squat to escape the splash and knocks a basket over in the mire.

- Have a care Lou! Mari snatches the basket upright and in doing so releases Morag who slides into a sideways topple towards the water. The mollieboy reaches and clasps and arrests her slow fall. Mari takes from the basket a vivid red berry-fruit slightly wizened and thumbs it hard between Mari's lips. - Chew. And swallow. Be sure to swallow it all.

Morag gulps and dry heaves.

- Good. And now the bodyshock.

By the oxters Lou and the mollie haul Morag upright and stagger with her limpness into the river. Mari follows. They all gasp. Morag struggles weak and clumsy as she is taken belly-deep. Over her drooping head Lou and the moll exchange a nod and at that they plunge Morag beneath the surface and hold her there for a count of ten. Her pale hands crane and beckon. Sloppily grasp air like the necks of grebes in a dance of courtship. Roaring she is raised. Another plunge for ten. Raise again and now she lolls and appears to have lost consciousness. Some red streaks now on her clinging smock. Thick streaks lumped with matter purple and scarlet. Chunks like limpets.

- Should I fetch a twig?

- No need, says Mari. - See the purge is on her. Out it comes now look.

Clots shoal away from the group and are carried downriver. Trails like heavenly bodies in their fleets across night skies.

Mari will not look at these pieces as she has never done and will never do.

- One more and it'll be done.

No force required for the third plunge; Morag is a sack now. Without resistance entirely.

On Sion's workshop floor lie iron spikes in a bundle like wooden faggots next to a hearth. Sion is holding another into flames in the glove huge on his hand like those worn by the hawk-handlers. He withdraws the spike now red and white at the tip of it and hammers it on an anvil. Turns it and hammers it again. Sparks jump and drift and wreck themselves against the apron that guards his torso. At a safe distance Ianto stands with a besom and observes. Each hefty clanging whack of the hammer putting a flinch into his face. Sion holds the spike up before his eyes and assesses and nods then puts it in a pail of water. Ianto hears an angered dragon.

- As hot as the sun, he says.
- That it is Ianto boy.
- As hot as the sun, he says again.

A blaring grotesque comes through the kitchen door; always the shock of his blunder and racket. The silver satin waistcoat straining against the gut-bulge and the swaying periwig and the clomp of the thigh-high boots and cane on the slate floor and the facial cosmetics thickly caked. Lips as red as a hollyberry and the caulked clog on the nose to conceal the craters of rot out of which Lloyd knows a whiff of whey will come should Sir Herbert embrace him which he does.

- Lloyd! Come here to me man.

Sir Herbert throws a scroll and a gold-tipped cane onto the table and wraps Lloyd in his arms. Lloyd presses his cheek into brocade to avert his nostrils from the other man's face and takes three steps back quickly once released.

- I see you have met Swinburne, says Sir Herbert, in his usual thunder.

- Just, yes.

- Just? Ah well then you have delights ahead of you. But be sure to latch the door when you retire. Sleep with an eye open and keep your arsehole stoppered with a cork, hah?

Sir Herbert winks and the artist Swinburne simpers and then Sir Herbert sweeps with a flitch-sized arm the still-life materials off the table and onto the flagstones. Making room for the spread of his scroll.

- Sir Herbert! A care! My still-life that was and arranged in the great particular! To catch the light!

- Whisht, Swin, and fetch me a drink by God. I have the soot of London Swinburne still in my throat hence a thirst to be slaked forthwith. A crate of sack in the conveyance there is. Bring it.

He points at the door and watches Swinburne as he leaves then unfurls the scroll and weighs down each corner with a potato. Beckons Lloyd to him to lean in close. - Here now Lloyd. Cast a careful eye.

- What is it sir?

- A blueprint.

- For what?

- What do you think, man? For profit as all such depictions are including the one you walk upon God-designed as it is. Augmentation of returns. Of capital investment. There is nothing else. Now, my man Beynon insists that he has knowledge of this very model here failing in the borderlands not a week since at a place called Rossett and burning four boys but I wonder.

Lloyd regards the marks on the scroll. - At what Sir Herbert?

- Come again?

- What is it you wonder at? Why should Beynon's knowledge err? What knowledge have you to gainsay his?

- For shite, Lloyd, must you be the death's head at the feast? Is there not another snug hearth-fire nearby that you can douse with your piss? And you catch my meaning in the wrong hand in any case. My wondering is for you to wonder at. Now regard. Look close.

Sir Herbert puts a finger on some words. - You see that there? The "Miner's Friend" it reads. What would you say it is at a guess?

- A pump of sorts. The lines I can decipher.

- But not the words. Nevertheless you are correct in your assumption. A pump indeed it is to carry water from one place to another and as it does so it frees more coin. Conjures more coin. Maximisation of profits Lloyd and there is nothing else. Know what I see in this? Seeing this through the eyes of the East India Company I am, an agent of which I am fresh back from visiting in the capital. The skill, the gift of men such as him to see in a lake or a mountain or a forest the monetary worth of every leaf or every crumb of soil or every drop of water. To traverse the globe Lloyd with such a talent bellying the sails, can you imagine? The ownership. The having of it all. Such a talent awes me man. Awes me. Truly it aims for the status of deity.

Sir Herbert passes his fingers across the scroll in a stroke. Almost reverential. - On which subject I must ask of my man Samuel. He's at his work I trust?

- He is.

- With success?

- That I cannot with any surety say. But see him out in all weathers and at all hours I do.

Sir Herbert nods. - Good.

- So is that you, sir? The Miner's Friend?

A laugh is barked. - Heavens Lloyd. You and I will talk out in the garden shortly and I will put my trust in you to the severest and most taxing test yet. Through a naif's eyes you yet see. Oh and tell me; did you through those eyes see Huw Twp on your journey over the hills to here?

Lloyd nods. - The sheep-fucker, aye. That I did. He dangles still.

Another bark. - Huw Twp fucked no sheep or not any of mine anyway. His sin against me was to stick fast in his hovel after he'd been told to leave. Have you me? You understand what I say to you? And know you why poor Huw is stuck fast in his cosy cage now and forever more?

Lloyd now and for the first time during this meeting regards Sir Herbert's face. The eyes and the teeth and the wens on the nose weeping through the powder. A tiny thing moves in the periwig and shows a jointed leg then retreats back into the thick white weave. A clink of glass outside the door breaks the moment.

- Ah the dauber comes with my drink. Artists, Lloyd, beware them and their futile skills that they in their enormous self-regard mistake for a wider and more valuable application. And beware this particular one Swinburne doubly for the man is a colossal pervert for whose pizzle no hole is bebarred, hear me clear. When wine is taken the man is insatiable. A ram. A tomcat. And endlessly entertaining for that. My jester he is and what personage of my stature would ever be without one. Look where he comes, the fond fool of mine. And keep your breeches tight.

Swinburne comes in through the door with his arms wrapped around green bottles.

- We'll talk later Lloyd you and I. On the lawn so. First I must swill London from my gullet.

At the far edge of the bone-field on the rise just below the tree-line and a small distance beyond the cluster of headstones crudely graven stand Lou and Mari and the mollieboy silently watching Dic Bach fill a hole with dirt. Wet and slobbery the earth flops off the blade. One naked toe protrudes still from the soil. One single toe only five feet or so distant from a tuft of hair. All that remains to the ever-grey sky and soon to be interred also. Some meatbirds in the leafless tree noiselessly and alertly agog for carrion. Two more scrapes each to cover the toe and the tuft and then Dic blade-slaps the dirt to flatten and Mari and Lou and the moll strew across the patch of turned earth some seeds and grasses. A y-shaped branch of a rowan. Dic leans on his shovel. Lou and the mollie hold each other and weep in the drizzle.

- Diolch Dic Bach, says Mari. - For both the internment and the confidence that I do not doubt you will keep, in what form will you accept payment? Coin or cunt?

- Needs be coin, Mari fach and alas for me to say so. 'Twould of usual be the other as you know but that pig-fucker Samuel is at his scavengings he is.

- Don't I know it. Mari hands Dic a coin. - There. So I will see you tonight when I'll wager that Lou will accept that back from you unless I miss my informed mark, yes?

Dic smiles and touches his cap and leaves with his spade over his shoulder like a weapon. Down the slope in which the bones have been sown long over. Generations interred in the soil and the blue clay beneath. Lou and the mollie break their clutch and come to stand alongside Mari and all three regard the turned earth at their feet. Lou pulls the cuff of her sleeve over her bunched knuckles and wipes her nose with it.

- From where was she?

- The north country I believe. Alba or its borderlands.

- And what God did she follow? Do you know?

Mari gives a small smile. - Why? You would address him now?

- Well, says the mollieboy. - It seems appropriate, no?

- If it be your notion that somewhere there are ears to hear you then by all means do so. No harm will come of it that I can foresee.

- Which deity but?

- Ach fuck, I do not know. The one of sluts and slammerkin and the poor. Whichever it has that has a face turned away. But haste it for low pit has shift-end shortly and too I have a longing for gin.

The mollie genuflects and kisses the knuckle of his thumb. Above him in the branches the meat-birds shift and flex their inky wings. Wind, greasy drizzle. The three people bow their heads in the smirr and some entreaty is muttered to the earth and the stones and the buried bones and the flesh-shells yet to be bone.

The sack on Sion's back clinks with each step and is mirrored in miniature by the one on the back of Ianto. The two of them in tight tandem. Pit-spikes in Sion's carry-all and their offspring nails in the boy's. What with the sacks and the similarity of gait Ianto could be Sion's fetch. The lesser get of him. They walk in the wheel-rut out of the settlement and towards the chimneys and pit-heads that crowd the nearby slopes and the lower skies and into the metronomic thump-clank of their dirge. Discarded machinery lies about rusting in its metals and rotting in its timbers. Broken cart-wheels and mounds of spoil in slumgullion puddles and the picked and begrimed ribcage of some large animal. The mud underfoot has been repeatedly strewn with crushed stone and cinders but the passing of boot and hoof and rim has driven such hardcore deep into the slime. In the guttering ditches at the sides of the track rubbish lies in heaps at one of which Ianto stops to point.

- Look Sion.

- What is it bachgen?

They stand and they stare. A ripped ewe belly up. Rent and the entrails gone from the cavity. Prised ribs an echo of the hole in the chapel's roof. A bone-cage for a nothingness. Flesh on the skull retreated from the long teeth and the socket's grub-simmering.

Ianto stares. Sion looks from the boy to the carcasse.

- Are you afraid of the wolves bachgen da?

Ianto shakes his head.

- You are. Have you frit they do.

- Only sometimes when it's dark and I hear them on the hills.

- That sound they make?

Ianto nods. - Like ghosts they sound they do. When it is dark. The demons that Preacher Evans speaks of that wait.

- Tis just wolves Ianto. The few that remain. Sion jiggles the sack on his back and walks away and Ianto follows him. - Soon the wolves will *be* ghosts they will.

Ianto does not respond.

- Nearly all gone they are now continues Sion. - One pack only remains they say and shortly that will too be gone.

And then you will not hear them anymore and you will not be afraid.

- Not of *them,* no.

- Not of them? Of what then?

Ianto does not respond.

- And now the sadness. What is it bachgen?

- I fear their wailings when they keep me from my sleepings or take a shape in my dreamings but I do not want them gone.

- Saddens you does it? These mountains without the wolves?

- I have heard them from my birth. Always.

Sion slaps at something on his neck. Gnat or midge. - And so you are sad.

- And still frit.

- Of what?

Ianto sniffles. - Of holes. Like I feel sometimes when I look down into a shaft and can see only blackness. Like the night sky but without stars or moon.

- So you are afraid of the hole that will be made when the wolves are all gone. Is that it?

Ianto nods.

- That is why they sound like ghosts you see because they know that they're going from this place, Sion says. - Crying they are. They do not want to go. Like the little people. Right to be sad you are.

- The little people? Like me? Ianto's eyes so big.

- No not you good boy. The cochyn. The pobl fach. All going from this place they are just as Edric Gwyllt said.

Blackened men pass one way and less blackened men pass the other way and the two groups move through each other and mingle for a moment then separately re-cohere again and apart. Across the slopes pony-drawn carts rock and somewhere machinery clanks and grinds. A stack burps fire. Atop a house-high mound of dark spoil stands Llew waving his hat for attention.

- Sion y Gof! Up here now! Bring the boy! Haste!

A film on skins. Greasy meniscus come from the air thickened as it is and plastering itself to bare integument and concocting knots in hair. Like a skin itself which indeed it is on the puddles and ponds across which small insects skate and skid. The call of lost lands in the re-shaped contours of tumuli and twmpath and peaks that once were islands. Gulleys along which great sea-beasts once cut. Commas of larvae flickering in the tiny pools of the bullawns into which reverent and trembling fingers are still sometimes dipped.

Against a circle of light Ianto is spread like a four-pointed star. Slowly filling that circle as he is lowered by rope further and deeper into the earth. On the surface above him Sion has braced himself with his feet against the lip of the shaft and with a rope looped and knotted around his waist that he inches out carefully between his whitening hands. Tautly it enters the earth. It thrums. Llew is prone at Sion's side to peer into the pit-shaft.

- Timbers boy! There should be timbers!

The mountain eats Llew's voice. A faint response rises from within:

- I cannot see! There is no light!

- Feel around! Use your hands boy! See by touch!

- Given him a lantern you should have, says Sion. - Or a wick at the least. He is not a cat Llewellyn.

Llew looks at Sion. - And nor is he a spider. Two arms only he has. Which he needs to touch timbers. He drops his voice back into the shaft. - What can you feel Ianto?

No answer. Llew shouts again: - Ianto boy! What can you touch?

- I feel one! Have it in my arms I do! comes Ianto's voice from the earth.

- Bachgen da! Tie it to you as I showed! Then, to Sion: - Haul away Sion y Gof. Heave him up now and we can begin a healing on that fucking chapel and piss on Lloyd's righteous fire.

- Up you come Ianto! Sion starts to reel the rope back in. Strain on his face with the added weight. The rigid neck sinews. He braces and pulls hand-over-hand and the slack coils at his side. Of a sudden his hands slip and the rope rips through them and his bellow is answered by the same from the shaft and Sion bites his lower lip bloody and re-takes a tight grip although there is now a redly livid welt across the back of one hand. He hauls. Llew assists. A tuft of Ianto's hair appears out of the hole and then his pale face and then the rest of him with his small arms locked tightly around a thing that is looped by rope around his neck and it is longer than him and about as wide and as filth-caked as he. Llew reaches out and takes hold of the boy's collar and scrambles him onto the earth's skin where he lies panting. The object lying aslant him. Sion squats.

- D'iawn Ianto? D'iawn my boy?

Ianto wipes his face. - Frightened I was.

- You did good. Safe you are now.

In a crouch Llew wipes some muck from the object.

- This is not wood. Not timber. Feels like nothing on earth nor in it.

Sion looks from Ianto to the object. The boy lies panting and prostrate. The frantic exhaust of him.

Sion and Llewellyn are yoked together as they carry the object on their shoulders. Sharing its weight. Seven feet or so between them so long is the thing in semblance of a gargantuan bolt with a loose nut at each end. A hinge from a gate of hell. Ianto follows behind and he is like a figure in a doorway with the object the lintel and Llew and Sion the jambs.

- Did I do good?

- That you did, says Sion.

- That we do not yet rightly know, says Llew. - We will discover.

In the shed the one-eared man rolls the object into the water-stream as Llew and Sion look on. Ianto stares at the hole in the man's head and the mesh of membranous strings in there as if a spider has crawled in and spun its web. The riddle shudders then fits and caked dirt sloughs away and the man wrestles the thing out of the trough and onto the stone floor and now cleaned it can be seen or largely seen because some petrification bulbously encases one end of it like a wart but the thing can now be recognised for what it is.

Llew reaches out to touch. - In the name of Christ.

The man jumps back and holds his hands to his head: - Ddraig! Ddraig mun!

Llew spits. - Have onto yourself Elis. Dragon indeed.

- Then what mun?

- I do not know. Sion?

Sion is cradling his scabbed hand against his chest.

- I neither.

- Aim a guess.

- I have none.

Ianto stares in wonder. - A big bone it is. From inside the mountain. Found it I did. From a thing too big.

The painting has progressed. Against a dark background the two carrots in a V and an allium that gleams as if with a light within. A brassica too. An apple. A throb and sap depicted in these and Lloyd and Swinburne stand and study and sip at glass beakers.

- First in what I intend to be a series of such Lloyd. A mere preliminary really. Still life.

- Still life?

- You are unfamiliar with the term?

Lloyd nods.

- A composition of this nature is referred to as a still life. I would solicit your opinion.

- Why? I am no painter.

- Of course not but these objects are your tools I would contend, says Swinburne. - Which you work with every day, do you not? When you are at this place at least. You sow them and you grow them and you pick them and we eat them. I have witnessed and with no small admiration I might add the care with which you apply yourself to such cultivation. So I would know whether they seem true to you as I have rendered them here.

Lloyd rubs his cheek. There is a rasp. - I am not certain what you mean.

- Well, the cabbage, for instance. Is it... to you does it appear...

- What?

- Well. Like a cabbage? Cabbagey?

- Cabbagey?

- Yes. Looking at its depiction, in the paint, can you sense the soil in its roots and the fluid in its veins? Does it look, ah, alive to you in my rendering of it, seeing through the eyes of a skilled groundsman as you do?

Lloyd nods. - In such a light as this yes. I would say it does.

- Such light? We can close the drapes.

- No no, the light in the paint is what I mean. The, the glow that you have worked into the pigment.

Swinburne's nod is almost satisfied. - Can you elaborate?

- I think not. Further words are beyond me. I do not own them. But I look to the shades here and the light that casts them or what you have made happen with the light. In the pigment.

- Go on. Swinburne tops up their beakers.

- When I take these things up from the earth. Not only then but for some time afterwards. When they are out of the ground they remain living. I feel them in my hands. Like birds or like lambkins. I cannot find the words.

- You're doing well. Continue please.

- I have not the words.

- If that is so then the reason is that you are searching in the wrong places. The words you uncover without breaking your brain are the suitable ones to use whatever they might be.

Lloyd looks once at Swinburne then back at the painting. - I mean that there is a, a beat in the hands when I hold these things. A pulse as from a heart. Have you ever held a thing newborn?

- An infant?

- Yes but not only of men. A lambkin as I say or piglet. They kick and they struggle before they settle.

- I think I understand.

- So do these things I take from the soil. Because it is like I bring them into the world.

- You are midwife to them? You help them into being?

- No, no. They already exist do they not? In the dirt. You cannot see them yet there they be. Already rescued from the void of unbeing.

Swinburne laughs. - "The void of unbeing"? You have better words than I Lloyd and there are many who know me as a poet. Where does a gardener find such a pretty expression?

- They are not my words. They are a preacher's. I quote from him.

- I do not intend to mock my friend but to express surprise and impress that is all. And not an insignificant flare of pleasure I might add. To converse with you is of benefit to me. Go on if you would. About life and unbeing and other grand concepts.

Lloyd's forehead is furrowed. — I'm saying that both of us help these things to be born. Me and you. Both of us after fashion.

- Me also? How might that be, pray?

- Well the image of these things. These objects. The image of these things is not these things. It is but the image of them. And yet.

Swinburne downs his drink and refills his cup. - And yet?

- It is like I can smell them as I look. Lloyd massages the rills from his brow with a grubby thumb. - The soil and the sap as you said. My nose responds in accordance it does.

- Ah. I see or think I do. So, removed from the earth in actuality and hung now and depicted as they are in the figurative, cup them in your hands if that were possible and they would struggle and they would pulse. Like a form of...?

- Life. Unmoving on the canvas but life nonetheless. Still life.

- HA! Swinburne smacks Lloyd on the back and drains and refills his beaker again. The smack has released a dust-puff from the weft of Lloyd's coat and the motes of it turn and twinkle in a sunbeam. Lloyd sniffs and there appears some sort of warring in his face. Pride or something like it struggling with embarrassment or something like it. A pinkness in the cheeks. Swinburne regards this with a grin then turns his gaze to his artwork as does Lloyd and they stand in silent contemplation for a long moment and then there is a crashing apart of the doors that open to the garden and there is then Sir Herbert swaying a little in all his loud alarum.

- LLOYD! I require your hands outside. Too your expertise. A belch bursts. - Outdoors if you will. Garden. Forthwith.

Lloyd snaps from his reverie and drifts over to Sir Herbert. Swinburne indicates his artistry. - Regard my work Sir Herbert. To hang in and enliven the scullery no?

- Yes yes yes man. Later I will inspect. Twill suffice I am sure but other matters now press.

He clasps Lloyd's shoulder and steers him through the doors and out into the brightness where on the crushed stone stands a cart attached to a shirehorse whose massive head is snuffling in a nosebag. On the bed of the cart and agleam in its bits is a disarticulated machine like a scale model of a city with its steel tubes and copper domes and thick rubber rings the circumference of the horse. Stacks of iron rods and spikes and triangular wedges. Sir Herbert points his belly towards it. The bulge of that belly all stained and sticky-striped and bestrewn with leaves and crumbs. He beams sloppily with his hands on his hips as Lloyd studies and touches. Fingers reverently tracing the components' smooth contours.

- And there she is, Sir Herbert says. - Of course awaiting assembly.

- The Miner's Friend.

- There you have it Lloyd. The Miner's Friend indeed. You have an eye.

- Recognise it from the design I do. The shapes.

- As I say you have an eye for more than turnips and leeks. Sir Herbert smiles in his whiskers. - Fresh arrived from the port. Each piece down to the smallest screw sucked money from me like a leech sucks bile so have a care.

Lloyd's caress is gentle. He smooths his hand across the shining copper.

- You will wrap each piece threefold in burlap before transport to the settlement and you will not whip the mules. Care is the word Lloyd. Care. Swinburne has expressed a desire to accompany you so he can paint the thing constructed and in situ but resist his entreaties you will.

- I will? Can I ask why?

- Recollect Beynon's report do you? How it "burnt four boys before they drowned" were his words I believe if not verbatim then near as dammit. You will not take the man's jinx with you Lloyd. Here he shall stay. Here with me.

Lloyd nods. From somewhere in the big house a gong sounds once and shudders the air and Sir Herbert takes a fob from his pocket to consult. - Luncheon. Punctual. Take it with me you will in the garden and you and I will talk.

- Thank you Sir.

- We need to talk, you and I.

They sit at a table beneath an ash tree's spread branches for the shade. The picked carcasse of a fowl congeals on a platter and bones gnawed and nibbled adorn Sir Herbert's jerkin. Empty bottles about. Sir Herbert dabs at his lips with a handkerchief in a curiously dainty fashion and then uses that cloth to wipe the moisture off his brow that has trickled down from beneath the powdered scrolls of his peruke. Lloyd scans for the reaching leg again but does not see it. For the past ten minutes Sir Herbert has uttered no words, stuffed as his mouth has been with flesh and drink and now he looks up from his trencher at Lloyd and tuts and reaches out to clasp Lloyd's cranium in one big hand and tip it to stretch the neck.

- Christ Lloyd. The mould has returned. The mildew.

He scrubs at Lloyd's jawline roughly with his kerchief. Releases his grip and examines the greenish smear on the silk.

- Look at that man would you. The filth. Have a caution and remember to scrub the settlement from yourself good and thorough prior to travelling here. This I have told you. Repeatedly. More stuff than deferential mannerisms come under the banner of respect for God's sake.

Sir Herbert's speech has lost its definite edges and blurred somewhat it is now. Lloyd rubs his neck and face with a meat-greasy hand and looks with gratitude to where a creature from marvel is crossing the lawn. The fever-dream of its tail in a train behind it. Out from the rhododendrons it has come.

- Still he looks for his hen, Sir Herbert says. - Pining my peacock is. Wolf took his mate some weeks ago and yet he seeks her still.

- Wolf you say? Not felid?

- Not felid no twas wolf. Saw it my man Beynon did and took its ear away with a flintlock ball or so he tells me. One inch lower and the cur's brains would've decorated my lawn which tells me only that the sooner we have eradicated the beasts the better for us all and that Beynon needs to hone his aim. Which reminds me. The settlement fayre. A firm date been set has it?

Lloyd gives the date.

- Good. By which time Beynon will be a crackshot. Sir Herbert gulps his drink and pours another. - He will be duelling at the settlement then.

- With whom?

- One sheep-fucker called Heslop. George Heslop. One who tested the honour of Beynon's woman and thus of course of Beynon himself.

- The dam of Sion y Gof? From the settlement? She who was chattelled to Beynon following the death of her spouse from the chokedamp?

- No. Beynon's woman is the innkeeper at Adpar. Who is this Sion y Gof?

- Metalworker in your pit he is. Your employee in effect. Of which I appreciate you have a very many and cannot reasonably be presumed to be familiar or even acquainted with them all in particular the lowliest. The mother of him was carnal with Heslop once if memory serves. Chattelled to him as she was.

Sir Herbert flaps a hand. - This matters not. Of no consequence is this. Beynon's bitch business is his own and the affairs of a vulcan whelp mean less to me than the dung with which yon bird has besmirched my lawn. Much more of it and I will hold the fowl across the chopping block and take its head myself. Tell cook to fire up the stewpot. With, with apricot and onion. Done it long since I would have were it not a gift from the Secretary of State a pleasure on the eye tho it may occasionally be.

Sir Herbert reaches for the bottle and sways a little in his seat as he does so. Pours a drink in silence. Shaken leaves cast trembling dapples across the table. Lloyd softly prompts:

- And the duel, Sir Herbert…?

- Ah. Yes. The duel. He drinks and gulps. - Day of the fayre. I plan to visit the settlement in any case to… to…

- Yes?

- To… to… for the purpose of…Sir Herbert's face folds into thought then lights up: - Yes! I hear there is a new whore! A silent one, begad!

- You hear true.

- The very best of whores! A silent one! I knew of one such in Llanidloes. Two years back or so. Made mute she was and oh such a blessing that she could not rot my ear with her 'plaints. Oh bliss! Silent in totality bar the gruntings and piggy squals that I…

He trails off. Lloyd prompts again: - And this duel of which you speak?

- This duel, yes. Beynon and the sow's cunt Heslop. In the settlement on the day of the fayre and I will have you as the second.

- The second?

- You heard me.

- I have no experience in such matters Sir Herbert. I would be useless in such regard believe me.

- I will believe what I believe man and what I believe is what I can with my volition bring into being. My boy Beynon's second you will be and I will countenance no contrary. I have and trust your loyalty Lloyd and that throws ability into shadow. In all walks of life. As it must. A terribly under-rated quality is loyalty yet the recognition and nurture of it and appreciation of what can be marvellously concocted from its very essence has stood me in good stead.

Sir Herbert drinks again, Refills again. Sees Lloyd adrift in consideration and bangs the table with his fist to startle. Things leap.

- Hoy! Attend closely Lloyd. Listen very fucking carefully to me now. Here I must test that loyalty.

A breeze tosses branches above. The petal bells of the rhododendrons nod and bow and behind them somewhere the peacock shrieks.

- A valley flooded Lloyd. Filled with water. This vision I have. The entire valley flooded and at its end stand ranked wheels turning endlessly each one powered by the pressure. Never-ceasing. The power. And the mountains roundabout chipped and nibbled away at no I have that wrong say *bitten* at or gnashed at. Chomped, yes, great chunks removed every day and processed every day until the mountain itself is grit no dust and then there is another mountain to be levelled and another valley to be flooded and on and on. A deluge again Lloyd but this one not from God's wrath but from his desire for his chosen ones to fulfil his work on this his creation. You have me? Hundreds of wheels Lloyd. Thousands. All turning turning. Industry the likes and size of which this country has never before seen. You have me? My vision. A lake so vast it must be crossed by ship yet this is inland. No sea but a sea it might well be. Spin my head does at the thought. Such things I dream of. This I see.

Lloyd gulps at his drink. Flicks at a picked bone on the platter. - I think I see. The Miner's Friend.

- Is the mine *owner's* friend. Ah Lloyd we are similar us two we are. I had contemplated explosives of late and indeed Beynon and I scoped the pool above the settlement to assess the viability of such but we are both of the mind that the risk of levelling the mountain is very real and very great so tunnelled is it. One blast to break the banks and the mountain itself could be pancaked and all the galena lost. And my vision too. My ambition alongside laid waste with that.

- So it will be pumped instead.

- That it will Lloyd. Clear you have it. A score of such machines will move the pool into the valley and my God Lloyd that notion in itself sparks a flare of the divine in me. The strength and the might to move lakes and flatten mountains can you imagine? The power. Colossus I will bestride this land. Straddle the new-made lake so huge will I be as to make it seem a puddle of my piss. A, a fucking giant I can be. A titan.

Lloyd looks up from the bones. - And the settlement?

- What of it?

- It will be drowned. If I am correctly understanding.

- Ah. Well. Here now we get to the trial of your loyalty. Sir Herbert drinks and re-pours. Thinks. Then: - I am giving such responsibility up to you. Such is the measure of my trust in you man. The extent and value of it. Channel Noah's spirit you can and how many other men are granted such an opportunity? Lead your people Lloyd. Deliver them from the deluge to come. Take them to dry ground and rewarded you will be with more than a bird-borne olive branch and a fucking rainbow begad.

- In what way pray?

- A share of the profits man. Dib you in on the deeds I will. The specific portion of which is to be further discussed and determined but for a percentage you most certainly have my word. Not to mention the reward in the world to come.

- I see not how I can shift the settlement entire. The houses. The people. The—

- In frankness Lloyd the buildings and the people are none of my concern. Their security is in your hands now and such is my gift to you. My conscience will be clear and unworried. Will yours? Answer that question well and twice the man you are now you will become. For certain.

Lloyd holds the lower part of his face in his hands. Speaks through finger-palings: - Sir Herbert I am being bent by these demands. Second Beynon. Uproot hundreds or have them drown. I am no dueller or woodworker and I cannot build an ark. Blunt here I must be.

- Well then you plunge me in disappointment you do. There is no insurmountability in these my offerings to you. I offer you my confidence and my trust and the golden opportunities for you to further yourself and to permit you to expand beyond the limits of your nature and nurture and to see you scurry away from such challenges issued from my largesse deflates me Lloyd deflates me. Strong shoulders to stand on I require and I had reckoned I saw them on you I did but how painful it is to recognise my error. The most prominent hindrance to the attainment of greatness is the smallness and diminution of the necessary assistance cruel irony that it is. Very well. I am sore disappointed more in the misdirection and misplacement of my trust than in the paucity of your own strengths but from this I will learn.

- No Sir Herbert you have me wrong, I—

- BAH! Sir Herbert makes a noise like a ram in rut. Swipes his kerchief across his face again with a roughness that removes some of the powder on his nose and reveals some of the red-ringed craters there. Small hollow pocks inflamed and weeping. - The fucking whining man! The whining! Like a whore used and unpaid you sound! Sweet Christ man you live in a moment of opportunity such as God has never bestowed such as mankind has never been given and you whinge and you wheedle and you whine! India. The New World. Every inch of these lands the brave are marking with their footsteps and turning the indigent savages towards the light and see fit to thank us soon they will and newly from London I am where I did hear talk of a further empty vastness far to the south where as yet no white man no chosen one has trod. A world entire to itself and what treasures it may harbour we do not yet know but all we can hope for and wonder at will be repaid if our prior ventures and discoveries are any guide. Adventures and riches demand men to suit them and such men are not those who sit there at another man's table full of that man's magnanimity and whinge like a mollieboy when tasked above their office. Yes man you deflate me you do. The treasures that await in places known and yet-to-be-known are too much for the mind of one man to grasp regardless of its greatness and they are all there for the taking of by the ambitious and the favoured. And think not this is a boon for the mere duty of it and the edification of the savage which burns at its core is one of the most awesome burdens ever to afflict civilised men and all we can take from the soils and the waters of these lands is purely recompense. Purify the primitives we do and at the discharge of that duty huge as it is the lands give gratitude to us. What do you think gold is man? Or diamond? Even the ore hereabouts or coal itself for Christ's sakes if not tokens of thanks? Constant and diverse are the offerings from the new lands that we through our intrepidity and courage do discover and the tempers of these times demand titans to honour them yet too many sit with bellies full of the victuals and sustenance so generously proffered by other and better men and whiningly 'plain like fucking piglets. Squeal squeal. Christ man where is your dignity. Embarrass me you do.

- Sir Herbert I—

- No Christ man I will hear no more bleating from you.

Evidentially my assessment of you was erroneous and for that I must rebuke myself from hereon in. Deflated I am by the poltroon I hitherto did not see in you and deflated by my own self additionally for the flaws in my perspicacity. Poor my judgment is. Sir Herbert drinks and flaps a hand at the noises that issue from Lloyd. Thumps his beaker on the table and up jumps the fowl carcasse. Pours again from the bottle. - This is the age of the brave Lloyd. Magnificent times for magnificent men. It is all there for any man to take has he the stones to do so which pitiful few do. Embodied in the East India Company the tempers of the time are in the ability to see a vast new land for the first time and assess its wonders of flora and fauna and the boons concealed in the earth to, ah, to have the glorious gift to read it all every mountain every lake every river. From the loftiest peak to each blade of grass to transmute it all into wealth. To look at a cliff and see coin stacked as high. That talent man. That gift. Truly wondrous and truly God-given and only on those deemed worthy. In your pusillanimity Lloyd you do in effect spit in the creator's eye. For shame man.

- I—

- Hush! Herbert holds up a palm. - Only five words can follow that pronoun Lloyd. Five words only from the very many that the riches of the tongue afford and they will be 'will do what you ask'. Yes? Enough clatfarting. Enough. Yes?

Lloyd sips at his beaker and wipes his face and offers up a small nod.

- Not in gesture Lloyd. Hear the words uttered aloud I will.

Another screech from the peacock. Somewhere behind the rhododendrons which were some years ago gifted to Sir Herbert from a traveller to a far land and under which Lloyd has oft struggled to coax vegetal life that is not rhododendron since. The beauty of its blooms has never been lost on him but nor has the conquering reach of its roots and its limbs. Already a sapling sweet chestnut has begun to wizen. Choked.

Sir Herbert cups his ear and leans across the table. - Hear the words uttered I will man. Waiting I am. Re-inflate me now. Say the words.

Lloyd regards the wreckage of the eaten bird. The small cage of the ribs and the remaining white fibres of flesh. The merrythought within like an archway, some portal. - I will do as you ask, he says, and the heft of his voice surprises even him.

- Hah! Sir Herbert claps his hands and leans back in his seat. Re-adjusts his periwig which has come askew. - I knew twas within you Lloyd. Knew it I did. And now my judgment is re-confirmed in its perspicacity I am again at ease. I will express my appreciation and gratitude to you now and believe me there will soon be a sensation dancing on your tongue that only a small select few on this island have ever shared. Or for that matter deserved.

He takes a small bell up from the table and shakes it. A maid appears at the scullery door across the lawn and is told to fetch the sweetmeats.

- A certain treat awaits you it does Lloyd. A sensation of taste like no other and that I can guarantee. Earned this you have.

He belches and sways and pours more drink. Laces his fingers across his belly.

- So now. Whisht and attend. The machine you will take to the settlement with the greatest of care and return here quickly with my man Samuel unless I see you at the fayre beforehand then for which I will advise you to become at least a passable pistoleer. The purchase of that machine has left a hole in my finances that I would plug and replenish as soon as is possible and so I require my legal taxes. Money like nature herself abhors a vacuum and will fill such with itself. Trial run my engine you will and appraise me of its performance. You have a query?

- The ah, the flooding Sir Hebert. The deluge you prophecy.
- What of it?
- Should I prepare? Should I announce its imminence?

Sir Herbert shrugs with both pumpkin shoulders. - None of my concern. All on you now this is. But declare I will that some time must pass before my vision can be realised. Require further equipment I do still. And I will have some notion of the efficacy of this particular model as commensurate with my wants. But the timing of your announcement and the commencement of the duties I have gifted to you is entirely on your shoulders. Those broad and capable shoulders of yours. But time does not press for now.

Lloyd's eyes for a moment slide shut. Behind them he sees a pearl-chain of bubbles escape an open mouth. A rank of thrusting engines in black outline on a ridge becoming a beach. A black expanse of flat water like oil.

The shaken maid appears with a tray. Her bonnet and blouse awry and a redness to her face.

- Straighten yourself girl. Show respect you will. Were you hauled through a hedge?

She curtsies and bobs. - Please Sir Herbert tis your man Swinburne I fear in drink he has become unmoored.

- Bah. Slap the man's face if he offends. Go back in there and administer a blow to the fool's face. You have my permission to do so.

She bobs again and deposits the tray and leaves backwards. In reverse. On the tray is a basket and a bottle of French brandy and in the basket is a large spiked thing with green serrated bayonets of leaves in a static explosion from the head of it.

Lloyd reaches out. - What on earth…

Sir Herbert harrumphs. - Forgetting yourself you are Lloyd.

Lloyd retracts his hand. - My apologies Sir Herbert. But what in God's name is that?

- I am told it is referred to as a "pineapple". It arrived on a clipper from the Indies I believe.

- It is like no apple I have ever seen.

Sir Herbert pours brandy for them both and removes from his pocket a knife and a snuffbox. Opens it to reveal a powder the hue of a setting sun. - And here a spice new come to us. Known as cinnamon.

- Sinnerman, Lloyd whispers, and taste the word he can. The exotica in it. All its suggestions. He watches Sir Herbert dig at the pineapple and strip it of its bark and cut away two yellow and dripping chunks and sprinkle them with the spice. Passes one on the point of the blade to Lloyd who takes it and has a ginger nibble. Thinks then says: - My God. My God.

Sir Herbert smiles around the colourful pulp in his mouth. - You see? Such rewards await you. Earn and deserve them man.

The kitchen door explodes outwards. The maid sprints screaming across the lawn with her bared breasts bouncing and with blood on her face and followed by a reaching Swinburne with his breeches ajar and his erection thrashing between the flaps of his shirt like an excited young animal. Sir Herbert roars and bangs the table with his palm. Bellows with laughter.

- Rewards, Lloyd! There they are! Rewards I say! Behold my clown! Priceless! Fucking priceless!

They drag the bone into the central square. The maes, if the irregular patch of dungy quag and detritus between hovels can be so termed and they prop it against the gibbet pole as if it awaits punishment. Men going to and coming from shift stop to stare and whisper and there is much touching of foreheads and hearts and genuflection and the forming of rings with thumb and forefinger to spit through thrice. Any hex to be defied. Men stand next to the bone for comparison and some children attempt to scale it and are chased away by Ianto protective and proprietorial towards it as he has become. It is his treasure and found it he did. The earth's remuneration for his bravery. Sion fetches a rope and Llew tightly secures the bone to the gibbet's stanchion against theft and he starts to charge to touch. Entitles himself as guardian to it and anyone close enough to do so automatically and seemingly without volition reaches out to touch and Llewellyn knocks the yearning knuckles with a stick. Soon enough Preacher Evans appears with his man Elis at his heels like a faithful hound and he approaches at a dash and slaps Llew's hand away when he canvasses for coin.

- Pay you Llewellyn? *Pay* you by God? I would as lief pay Satan himself man and you standing here to do the fiend's work for him. For shame and damnation eternal man. Do you but know it you gather the toll here for Hades.

Llew smiles. - Oh pregethwr. Understand that I love and worship and thank the Almighty for a thousand things I truly do and one of which is His refusal to call me to the cloth as he did yourself. Believe me.

- Oh I do man. I do.

Evans glares at Llew from beneath the brim of his hat. The slice of shadow there. He then spits on the bone and turns and his man Elis mirrors all movements in detail. Turns with his master to face the gathered crowd maybe a score in number, male and female and adults and childer both and each one ratty and wretched and rag-clad the lot of them amassed and uneasy in the grey and greasy air. Some dogs dart between legs nervously and a wire-haired terrier cocks a leg on the bone.

- You see? Evan's voice is big. - The cur alone amongst you knows what to do with such maleficent trickery. Piss on it. Afford it what all such dark deceptions are worth. From within the earth this came am I correct?

He looks to Llew who still smiling raises his chin at Ianto, who says: - Found it I did. Went in the mountain I did and took it out.

- Of course you did boy young and susceptible as you are for is not an open and unsullied heart the easiest to enter and the most rewarding to corrupt? Too the most tempting by far, by far. The preacher turns back to re-face the crowd. As does Elis. - Yes there are bones in the earth and the charnel in which you people toil or cleave to someone who does is your office. So up you come with the stone and the forebear's bones which when flesh-clad called you all. Held you. Bones you know and which know you. And told you I have from my pulpit of the Nephilim in the chapel which now stands punctured.

He stands silent. A smirr appears and swirls. Arms across his chest and a steady drip from his hat-brim. Some grumbles squirm through and out of the crowd.

- Told you I have time and time over of the giants that were once in the earth and of how the daughters of men met and knew the sons of God and mighty issue they did bear which grew yet larger in their mischief and did promulgate such wickedness in the soil and these are words you would do well to note: in, the, earth. And so God did see and every thought of his heart was of the evil done without stint and continual. Told you this I have time and time over. And sore it did repent Him that He had made men on the earth and such was his decision to destroy such creation from the earth's anguished face. So spake He. For it grieved Him that he made man. Made you.

He and Elis point at the crowd. A hawk squeals somewhere up above. There is coughing and spitting.

- And so in His fury He christened you Gibborim. In His holy rage. And set His son to see the strength that could be which He saw once and now could see polluted. Such wizened windfall apples His glorious creatures had become and now this here is His message. It is.

The preacher slaps the bone to bring a gasp out of Ianto and then he wipes clean his palm on his coat as if to rid it of taint.

- This here is His proof. The deception. Into mine ear come mutterings of beasts that were here before us as if we were not created alongside the world as if it was not made in totality for us alone in His image. Blasphemous talk there is, disgusting talk there is of us emerging from apes yes apes and before them even the lower forms that do writhe and wallow in filth. A word for this there is that I will not dignify through utterance because it's true name is trickery and Satan's toy this object is. Or rather you gathered here to gawp and touch idolatrous and unasinous are the toys and this object is the instrument with which the dark one plays you. Your eyes I do see empty of all but awe at a falsehood.

Evans shakes his head in a sadness deep. - And so does the Prince of Lies notch up another triumph. Hear his cackles I do. Look to yourselves and read the Book or have it read to you. Clean the soles of your boots for see them soon I expect to do oh yes. Give yourselves over to the matter and substance of your lives and turn away from falsehoods. This I am tired of telling you. Re-inter this monstrosity and return it to its sinning giver concealed from the eyes of childer or better still pound it to dust in the crusher with the ore. Behold and look upon what your antique gods have become. Look at it now and here it is. Go now and repent. Shrive. Offer your sorrows and save yourselves from flame.

He throws his arms open in abrupt and adept dismissal then turns his back on the crowd with Elis in reverent mimicry. The mist becomes rain and the crowd begins to disperse.

- My roof Llewellyn.

- What of it?

- Holed it remains as you fully know. The good folk deserve dryness during worship which is now evidently a matter of some urgency agog to temptation as they are showing themselves to be. And your man Lloyd promised me fine timber.

- Twas timber I was seeking when I found the bone.

- I found it, says Ianto. Ignored by the preacher.

- This I swear pregethwr, says Lloyd. - Sent the boy into the old pit I did to fetch the pren I know to be down there and re-surfaced he did clutching this.

- And what did you expect man? If you send a boy into the pit? The pit, if I need to repeat the word. Redolent as it surely is.

- Yes redolent, says Elis.

Llew has a hand on the bone as he meets the preacher's eyes.

- What lies in the pit Llewellyn? What awaits pure hearts in the pit? In God's name have I been wasting my breath these years gone? Or perhaps I speak in a tongue unfamiliar to you. Tis not frequently I see your face on the pews but Christ, man, Christ.

He coughs and spits and sleeves his face and makes a noise of exasperation.

- Gah. This infernal rain. The shrivelled souls about. Patch the chapel roof man and get rid of that. He nods at the bone. - Keep it out of all sight including your own. I would recommend returning it to the earth in the form of cinders but in what specific manner you dispose of it is your concern and decision entirely but hide it from my flock you will. Abet idolatry I will not do and nor should you man. Never.

Again he aims spittle at the bone and Elis does too then he walks some hurried steps away before spinning on his heels and returning. Elis is buffeted and confused.

- Think of this as a nursery Llewellyn. You, there you stand with a child and a twpsin. How can you not see that? As you would keep death from the mines to the best of your ability so you should keep temptation from a nursery. Think, man.

- Think man, says Elis, and he scuttles after the preacher. Llew and Sion watch them retreat and Ianto wraps his arms around the bone to tightly squeeze. Llew coughs and spits.

Falls the rain and fills the transh with a torrent and sets the wheel to shuffle and shunt. Men emerge blackened and blinking from portals in the earth from where comes the sound of hacking and hammering and above them the thin chimneys burp weak flames at the bruising sky. All struggles these dawns.

Return the day and lighten my heart even as these my hands start my fire. My forge. From the light inside me and out through my hands into this my hearth and forge. From which to hammer the utensils and such that afford men work and coin. So the light in the sky and in my breast does this. See this. And then the work begins and the coldness becomes.

Dandelion seeds and wisps of wool and puffs of downy breast-feathers lift and carry on the breeze. Smut-phantoms, memories of sparks. Lift and fall and twirl and briefly settle to be blown abroad again and soon. Yanked skywards in the dying blastwaves of hill-breaking explosions which throw up and bestrew bones and pebbles both in far-gone fog adorned with lightning bolts and concentric circles. Lines that echo animals and birds. Offerings of a sort or indulgences. Expressions of other and older bursts.

On the packed earth floor of the workshop lies the bone. Flamelight yellow on the curves of it and the huge calcified wart at one top-heavy end. Alone with it is Sion and at his work of holding steel spikes to a grindstone in a fierce spurt of sparks. A loose and filthy rag partly covers the weeping rope-burn on his wrist and the back of his hand and this rag could be a greasy wisp pulled from the coasting sky.

And I think it not like he said no the preacher-man in his cape. Stood like a meat-bird he did with his little familiar the Elis man like the small beasts the old ladies attend. Groundfall apples he said and yes but from there he went wrong he did because I did hear weeping. I have always and oft heard the weeping I have. A sadness more big than the mountains. Labour to make more we do for the big man Herbert and the smaller man Samuel and how all big men need the littler ones by their sides. How that is. Like my father to die so that others can wallow and like my mother to sicken and shrink and finally flee so that others can grow fat or fatter like the big rocks and not move and most do need the blasts to shift them. And that is the weeping it is because there is no weeping down here. Or there is.

He lets the steel spike clank onto the pile of others such at his side. Takes up another. Pumps the whetstone wheel with his foot. Sets steel to stone again and the lightning-white sparks gush.

And as there is no fish no more in the waters here inland so there is none of this heat I make in the people around. The red bellies of them little fish I used to love and they in the nests of their making beneath the water oh yes them fire-bellied little fishes did make nests down under the water like the birds do up in the trees and how I was marvelled by that as everything was but now no more no. Gone now and soon to be followed by the wolves I have not seen no never seen yet heard them so many times I have beneath moons of different colourings and sizes and up on the ridges they make their songs and soon be gone they will like it all like this bone they will be one day soon and that day is here now because these men about are not like them red-bellied fishes they are like this bone. Walk around on the earth they do but dead they are yes.

He drops the spike. Takes up another. Pump and press and grind. Sparks.

Like the little people as Edric Gwyllt said that when they go they do take everything else with them. Bisssssssson maybe that bone once was those tales of beasts that Edric does tell. Horse-big brock and cow-big cat. So big that people to them are what the mice are to my grymalkin and where is he now. Hunting is he. Everything is going and the dying is all around. GO. Where is my cat.

Sion lifts the spike from the turning wheel and looks about him and sees his cat on the bone. The delicate paws and the tail curled and the fiery eyes regarding.

Everything is dying my grymalkin my friend. GO.

Two mules to the cart heavy as it is laden with the machine in disarticulation. Each piece roped around and secured with knots the size of a bull's knuckle. Wheezing the mules and trudging without respite and Lloyd alongside them with his hand on the copper dome to stabilise yet still it rocks and yaws as the mules ascend a ridge.

- Steady. Steady. Easy now.

He raises a thin whipstick but stays his hand. Ahead of him and atop the hill like a veil hangs the oily gauze of a sleetcloud. Beneath it the settlement stews Lloyd knows as he returns to it with the disassembled components like an agent of anti-creation. As a chaperone of a messenger who has calculated and enacted the reversal of the world's natural bend towards progression.

- I almost dropped him Catherine. Almost dropped him down I did.

- And yet you held on cariad.

Catherine swabs the burn on Sion's hand with a damp rag. He hisses air in through his teeth. Red and rawly angry in the firelight from his forge is the wound and oozing ichor thick and clear. Some scabbing starting to form at the frayed edges. Like one of the deep wheel-ruts that score the mud outside.

- Taste again I did the eggs I had had. Up in my gullet again they came.

Catherine smiles. - Yet keep it within you you did and held on to my boy you did. I know you Sion y Gof; sooner be taken down into the pit yourself with him than let him drop alone no?

- But brave is your boy Ianto. Not me. Into the hole he went like a spider. Watched him do it I did.

She dabs the wound dry and gently wraps a strip of cleaner cloth around it and ties it off with a tug.

- Ow.

- I am sorry. Now keep this clean you must remember. Protect it from the dirt you must do. Seen such wounds go bad I have and swell like swine stomachs with the croup and stink and burst in foulness. What vulcan would you be with the use of one arm only?

Sion studies his dressing. Catherine holds each of his hands in hers, the bandaged and the nude. She examines the older healed burns and scars and nicks both healed and fresh and reads the narrative traceries in them. The imprinted tales. She releases his hands.

- Market soon. Go I must to ready.

- For what?

- The market Sion as I say. Berthed at the port a ship has and Mari and her ones will be plenty busied.

- Yes but what have you to prepare?

- Mari will have her mascots at such times. Her corn dollies and mommets and the like to gather guard against pollution like your cloth. She hopes one day to buy passage with their sale or barter.

- She does?

Catherine nods and the fire spits.

- She hopes to sell a great many then, says Sion. - A million.

- That much is true or must be. More than stars in the sky sufficient to pay for passage. Yet she dreams still and hopes.

On such ships. Oh afloat and nothing of the dread deeps beneath that carry and that claim.

In a short silence Sion looks at Catherine. The face of her in the dancing flames.

And what does each new puncture release. Each cut or burn from rope or fire or mere rip in the skin. What released and what let in. Like wants like said Edric the Wild.

- We can journey Catherine. Us two together. If you would like.

- Us? And how? For shite Sion I have a concern and a

spouse and childer. And no coin. Journey I cannot with you or without.

- No. Not like how you think.

- Then how? Swim would we? Fly? Did you knock your noggin in the rescue of my boy?

Sion reaches under his workbench and withdraws a cloth bundle. Unfolds it to reveal a variety of fungi. Thin brown be-nippled stalks in clusters and larger caps red and spotted white.

- See here Catherine. Tickets for passage of a type these are.

- Such colouring means 'beware' it does Sion y Gof. The red ones. Such colouring says 'do not eat me'. This I know.

- Not all of the time no. Only sometimes. For I have learned a method to prepare. We can go a-journeying Catherine you and I.

Catherine sits on the bone and observes as Sion tongs a small black-crusted bubbling kettle out of the fire. She pats the bone with a palm.

- A passable seat this is if nothing else.

- Llewellyn will have it at the market he told me. To display it is what he said. Charging to touch it he was in the maes.

- And people paid?

- Some did yes.

Catherine strokes the bone. - My father would unearth such things sometimes he would. Would talk about seeing them too. There was a pit full of such he said. Over the hill to the east.

- Which pit?

- Long filled now. Empty of treasures excepting these objects if treasures they can be termed. Just tir pwdr now in the main.

- And had he a notion of what they might be, your father?

- Bones such as this?

Sion nods.

Catherine shakes her head. - That he did not but they were to be shunned was his advice. Left in the earth or interred again. Saw no good in them he didn't although what otherness he did see he never made expressly clear. Not to even be seen much less discussed was the flow of his opinion.

Sion decants fluid from the kettle into a beaker. - And you? What does it say to you if anything at all?

- It makes for a passable bench as I said. I will make a wool sheath for it and we will have it as a settle.

Sion passes a beaker. A broth in it scummed with fungal twists floating brown and soggy-boiled.

- And we drink this?

Sion nods and blows on his own beaker to cool.

- Like slurry it stinks. And we will journey you say?

Sion nods and sips. - Of a type. Many times I have journeyed on this cawl.

-To where?

- To places far off. Drink and come with me Catherine.

The men screw and hammer and slot. Lloyd sits on a tree-stump with the blueprint on his knees and looks from it to the men and back again. Coming together is the engine. Taking on a shape. Ratcheted and riveted and bolted together piece-by-piece and the men busy about it like ants. Lloyd looks up.

- Kernow.

The big man turns. - What?

- You have it wrong man. Wrong end.

Kernow carries the steel rod he is holding to the other side of the copper dome. Blank and gleaming there it is like the eye of an insect immense.

- No man! The wrong end of the, of the shaft!

Kernow moves back and turns the rod around in his hands.

- Pig shit in that skull of yours.

- There is? Kernow points the shaft at Lloyd sword-like.
- Civil tongue. One warning alone Lloyd.

- Tis a valuable machine man. Make baubles of my ballocks Sir Herbert will were it to malfunction. And exact a large tax from you I might add. He is to put this engine to great matters.

Kernow slots the rod into its housing. Slaps it home with a palm and gives Lloyd a glare.

- What now man?

No response. Kernow turns away.

Outside Sion's furnace Catherine is all-foured in the mud. The vomit cataracts from her thin and bilious and abundant. Ribbons of it swinging from her underlip.

- Poison. Poisoned I am by fuck. Like a rat. Why Sion?

Lazy smile on Sion's face. Catherine looks up at him with her hair in cables across her face and her eyes full of horrored hurt.

- Why Sion?

- It will pass. Sion's voice is a drawl. He lolls against his workshop wall. - Always this happens the first time. Always but it will pass. Soon I will see you on this side.

Catherine's bowed back bucks.

Tall as a man and a man again it stands. The great compound eye of the dome bejewelled with water-drops on blocks a-straddle a cavity and entubed to a derrick like a keeled-over 8 against the colour-drained sky. The name NEWCOMEN engraven on a pipe. A further pipe links the derrick to the earth by way of the umbilicus of a pithead. Like this engine has been born direct from the earth. Or lays eggs within its skin through an ovipositor. Or is feeding, sucking blood parasitical. The men stand in a rough circle in silence as if in reverence to a constructed god.

And in the sepal of a flower sprouts a stamen cluster. Dots of pink atop a forest of smooth stalks. Something sees. Catherine sees. So small and so huge. Massive in her eye this tiny thing of delicacy so close is her face to the bloom. The purity and the grime embedded adjacent. So close. And the eyes on her huge and wild in such a hungry visual gulp. Voracious like that and gnashing for input.

- My God. Her voice is a whisper. - My God. Never before seen. Around me all days all the days of my time here my life and never before seen like this I see now.

- Who will descend?

No man answers and Lloyd repeats the question. - I said who will descend?

- You will Lloyd, says Kernow. - As an example to your men.

- Twas I who brought the fucking thing over the mountain from Y Plas was it not. You will go Cornishman.

- I would lick a sow's cunt rather than descend.

- It is an order.

Kernow laughs loud. - Oh an order is it? Be fucked Lloyd. Too much in Sir Herbert's company you have been.

- Tis filled with the watta. A voice from Lloegr's northern

parts sounds out from a rough red face. The cranium naked and the chin bedraggedly hirsute.

- And what use would a pump be without water to pump, Webb? Tis the entire point of it is it not? Cah. Lloyd coughs and spits. - Who will descend? Repeat myself as it seems I must.

No man responds. Then someone bleats: - Two good men that shaft took Lloyd year last it did. Drownded them it did. Filled their bodies with the cold slumgullion and two the year before too. Tis hexed it is.

- Which is precisely why we've here and now built that fucking machine, says Lloyd, is a voice raised and reedy.

- Cursed be buggered. Christ man that engine's operating record is completely clean and unsullied and virgin pure it is. That model it saves and that is what it's for. The very purpose of it. The workings at Rossett were taking three good men per week prior to the acquisition of such a device or so I've been reliably informed. Will none of you trust to progress and descend? Hexed be fucked. Who amongst you has the trust? Who has the stones of suitable size?

No response. Lloyd gives up a sizeable sigh. Pulls a coin from his pocket and holds it up to capture the weak light.

The underside of a black beetle is the design from an architect's dream fevered and fabulant. Maybe a Mulciber. A marvel pure. Up-ended the little creature kicks on Sion's palm and in each tiny moving joint is an endlessness. The legs intermeshing. So many moving and interlocking parts to this tiny thing and each dependent on each to fit flawlessly and seam all into one to bring the wonder of this being onto Sion's palm onto the earth from which it and all of it came and comes. Sion and Catherine study in silence. The two breathings of them. They watch the beetle right itself and split its carapace into lace wings in a monumental application of magical insect will and as one they flinch and gasp as it lifts whirring into the air. They watch it get taken smoothly away on the invisible thread that leads back to all beginnings and forwards to all possible ends and like children again they are or like no child itself has ever been. Or perhaps like they'll be at the moment of extinction and their senses ravenous before the snuff.

It is Webb who descends. Who goes into the earth with a rope around his waist. On his arse and sliding down the slope feet first into the shaft beneath the pump with his hands braced on the oblique walls. His panting bounces back off the wetly gleaming sides of the shaft and accelerates as he is taken deeper in and then breaks into a whoop as his bare feet touch with a tinkling splash the water colder than ice.

Amongst trees they stand. Sepulchral and cathedral-like. The sky sliced and separated by the branches above and around and the sigh of wind through the trunks. Faces in the bark appear for a moment and raise their eyebrows and then go. Catherine raises a hand to her face and flexes the fingers anterior to her eyes.

- Look Sion. Look here. She is whispering. - See the bones within I can. My God I can see my bones.

Chin-deep in fluid and securing his head above its surface via a tight grip on the tube that links the fluid to the circle of weak light above and seemingly so very far away. Webb grinds his teeth and spits and gags oily ooze rancid from his mouth. Floundering he is at panic's edge. The shuddering of his breath bouncing back off the wet carved walls. He tugs on the rope once and waits then tugs on it again with further force and up above on the earth's skin machinery jerks and thumps into operation. Rattles and then roars. In Webb's hand the tube starts to throb and writhe serpently and the water of a sudden drops below his chin. To his neck then chest then sternum. He yells triumphant, his teeth and eye-whites faintly luminous in the murk.

Like blossom the small white winged things fall and drift or like snow. Flakes of it aflutter around their faces rapt. Pure white the wings and tiny dark traceries in each like miniatures of trees. Veins perhaps to transport whatever these beings have for blood. One settles on Catherine's outstretched and quivering fingers.

These things. My heart.

- Such things, says Sion, and Catherine looks to his face.

- Like I have swallowed them it is. Like many of them are here in this my stomach.

In his tone and expression there is a suggested plea of some kind. Catherine looks back to her outstretched hand again and the astonishment on there with the wings slowly flexing.

They haul him out in his all-body slime caul and the machine rattles and heaves up brown liquid. They slap him on the back.

- Shekkiin lahk a shittin cur Ah wuh!

Above them the derrick nods and bows to each side and the water comes from it in thick spurts.

And Sion and Catherine laugh. On the bare hillside they regard each other and the known part of the world about them and the laughter leaps from them unfettered. For a long time they do this. A decade gone in a day. The settlement below them on the valley floor in this scatter and sprawl and a new noise arising from it like the gulping heave-breaths of a colossus newborn.

Scarlet scores the ridges. Sun sinking beyond and with all of it turning on itself. The small and human brains accepting again the balance of their chemistry and their reactions and the sparks that are sent and caught and the hue and the heat of the furnace high above.

Catherine declares that she must go and Sion does not respond so she repeats herself:

- Go I must now Sion. Children and miners to feed there are. Pretties to make for Mari.

Sion does not respond.

- And coin to count. For Samuel.

Sion now nods. - But journey again we will.

- Yes Sion. We will journey again.

They both stay seated on the lichen-spotted stone.

And back I am. Back we both have come. From somewhere very far away and where I already wish again to be. What lies behind almost to touch. So close.

Black birds nailed to posts and palings. Some see as messengers or harbingers or the departed souls of people in newer forms now damp and tattered black rags in a row. Dead feathers ruffling in the wind and the black beaks hanging agape and the eyes and their baggage long gone.

At his seat at the throat of his grotto sits Edric carving with a honed bone markings on a flat black disc of stone. Overlapping V's and other apatropaisms to keep him safe in his solo slumberings in the mountain's maw from whatever freed force that might seek redress which he knows there are and do for heard them he has. Seen them he has. Called from the howlings within the hills and the forms of men in rockfalls where real men once died and rotted their matters. And way way in back of them their far far distant fathers making homes in there themselves to huddle behind fires against the great and creeping shapes of each and every night. The starlight the moonlight given back from green eyes. All the gruntings. The boulders heard overturned and the trees toppled by force. Around Edric's dusted face now whine tiny biters and he twitches his head to dislodge and shakes the sprigs plaited into the hairs of his head and his face. The low words leaving his beard's brambles, a voice beseeching from a faraway shore across a maelstrom in soundless roil:

- So very far away. Beyond the horizon and then the further horizon when the first one is reached and passed. Snapped shut to us all is any heaven like the jaws of a gintrap yes. Tell them all but would they listen. So thirsty am I. Do they fucking listen. Water I see and collapse I see and hear I do the little ones in the throes of their final going. Their protest so fierce and they do not want their doom because with them goes an everything.

Is carried away with them. When he goes will the final wolf or will the final felid cry louder than all the others that have gone before? That have been taken before them? Will they know? And if they will then what fucking weight. What fucking weight.

For a beat Edric looks up from his work at nothing in particular or one single droplet passing through his vision. At no particularity or at a great particularity. Unfocussed entirely or focussed so intensely as to set a fire ablaze at its spark.

- Such last agonies. Claws that claim. From here on is this land and all the world's lands so many I have seen and walked upon and the ending has been embarked upon now it has. Set sail and headed we are for the end just as the ships I once boarded were bound for one place only and only the duration of the passage was unknown yet could be estimated just. Like the hooked draw that links the fish to the hand. Unstoppable that ending is as we have set a course in its direction and even those who wish it devoutly will miss it entirely which is to be dreaded most of all. Dreadful most of all. Fare-thee-well you little ones you pobl fach. There are no new forms for your return to take so this is forever. You have gone. Goodbye to it all. A great wave I see. A flood I see. Told them I have time and time over that evil does not and cannot exist until it finds a form to inhabit. One that is open to its infection. That welcomes it in. Only then can it come into being but would they fucking listen.

He holds his stone up to his eye. Squints at the scratchings he has made. The little sigils unreadable to all except himself and the murmurers in the dank winds that without respite still seek his throat.

Metallic scatter of coin across the tabletop lit by one tallow candle. Small suns the coins seem in their burnished metals. Small weak suns. The bronze and the silver all dulled and catching only a little light. Catherine picks through them and arranges them in little towers. A vast weariness scraped into her features.

- Forty-eight *fucking* farthings. She makes some marks on a slate with a sharpened stub of stone. - Twelve *fucking* pennies. And one *fucking* shilling.

She stops and gazes at no particular point in the room. A largeness moving through her eyes like a ship's sail big-bellied by wind. She shakes her head and returns to her task.

- And twenty-one *fucking* shillings to equal one *fucking* guinea.

More scratchings on the slate. More coins selected and arranged in a separate stack.

- One *fucking* guinea. Ten *fucking* farthings. *Twelve* fucking farthings. *Fifteen* fucking farthings and Christ this *fucking* boredom will surely kill me.

She moves to the windowsill and takes up the bottle resting there and unplugs it and takes a deep draft. Hears voices outside the room and beyond the walls getting louder and footfalls too and then Lloyd enters the room with Samuel and his armed guard in mid-conversation.

- Like a dream it does work Lloyd is saying. - I have the report reliable I do. Dust-dry that pit is now and will take no more men mark me. That I can guarantee. Move water in a mass it will and quickly I have no doubt and with more of the likes of it, well. Sir Herbert will have his visions realised. Mark you me. I doubt it not.

- This will please him, says Samuel.

- That it will. Lloyd looks to his spouse. - I have returned.

- That I can see. When?

- Been taking stock I have and working on machinery of great import and matters relevant to such. He takes the bottle from Catherine and sucks at it then offers it to Samuel who shakes his head.

- Not whilst at my function. The collections require a clear head. For the counting.

He strides to the table and regards the coins.

- I have not yet finished the reckoning.

Samuel sniffs. - Regardless of that Catherine this here is underweight. Scales unnecessary I can cipher that with my eye alone.

- Take what is there then.

- That I will do and let me hazard a guess: "next week". Hit my mark do I?

Catherine just stares. Fingers hair behind her ear. Samuel sweeps the coins into a bag. The tiny city all toppled.

- Very well. The last time I excused your tardiness was conditional on the gift of a fowl do you recall? Partridge I believe of which the wife was very fond. Most toothsome was her verdict. So take you your fowling-piece and I will return at sundown of the fayre. And I will relay the good tidings to Sir Herbert, Lloyd, viz the Newcomen.

Samuel and his guard leave. Lloyd takes a draw from the bottle and returns it to Catherine.

- Underweight?

She drinks. - That surprises you?

- On this occasion it does.

- For why?

- Has a ship not berthed lately in the port?

- Not yet.

- Been told it has I have.

- If it has then the men from it have not crossed the mountain as yet. The timing is not good Lloyd.

- Which excuse will not re-imburse Sir Herbert.

- Re-imburse him for what? Beyond his leech taxation I need not add.

- There is an engine. A pump. Not an hour since I saw it put to work with great success. Part of Sir Herbert's grand schemings it is any detail of which I will not divulge. To secrecy sworn I am. Sir Herbert paid for it and he will have his recompense and raise a tax temporarily.

- Another increase then.

- A temporary one as I said.

- Just like all the others before. Samuel has taken all I have and he cannot take what is not mine to surrender.

- Then you must make more.

- How Lloyd? Tell me how.

Catherine drinks and hotly stares and Lloyd takes in the room and the stuff in it. The naked table and the guttering candles and the mould-mapped walls. The bareness of them behind their growths. The infant asleep in a wooden crate beneath the table.

- Mari has lost a woman I have heard.

- What?

- That is what I've heard. Accepting fresh mops she is now. Soliciting for such even. A voiceless one even newly arrived I hear.

- And your meaning is?

- That you have something to hire do you not? An item for which men will pay and yet it will remain yours.

- That which I sit on. My placket.

Lloyd says nothing.

- And what allowed your children into the world. Your children.

Lloyd picks at a fingernail. - All of whom need to eat. We must make more coin.

- "We"?

- We. And I must go now to seek Llewellyn. He moves towards the door. - Think on what I've said. And remember Samuel's fowl.

He leaves. Catherine hurls a curse at the door. The candle-wax spits.

Along the line of crucified birds she moves. Poking each with a finger. At her touch the third corpse ruptures and releases a tumble of stink and maggots and this is the one she rips from its staple and enwraps in a rag and takes away with her.

From hovels and holes hacked from rock they come. From cavities in the trunks of trees and from pits in the earth they appear. Hutches of scrap wood and discarded storage tanks. From anything in which dwelling places can and have been hewn they emerge squinting even into this insipid sunlight. Skin greenish with mildew and a milky film across the eyeballs. All hair massed and matted and tangled through with the stuff of plants. Small bones in some. From behind a cataract one does come with horns of hair the colour of dirtied snow tallowed into an upcurving tusk on each side of his face and leading by a whip of hide a humanoid figure that scrabbles on all-fours like a dog alongside wheedling and growling also like a dog. A penwan; a gimp; a means to make coin on the days of market and fayre and a supplier of meat at other times.

The peculiarity of this pair skidding and loping down scree to the furthermost outskirts of the settlement where four stakes have been pummelled into the earth and bound round with spiked wire.

In the square the Frenchman slumbers against a crumbling wall with a felt slouch hat over his eyes and enwrapped in a stiffened blanket. Three urchins circle him and jab him with sticks to make him shift and grumble. Harder they poke in the thighs and ribs. One thrusts his spear into the Frenchman's cheek and produces a roar and a lash of the hand:

- Ne touchez pas! Cauchemar! Fuck off!

And the children's laughter scurries away with them. And market day is here and a ship has docked in the port beyond the mountains the sailors from which are filing over those mountains towards this rough square and its rough commerce. Small mounds of wizened vegetables for sale or barter. Eggs from diverse birds. Oozing sheets of flesh on slates and wooden trenchers and corn-dollies and patched rags and cooking pots once broken and now mended and re-nailed boots and knobbly candles and vats of caustic alcohol made from obscure raw materials and all of it is for sale. By the gibbet the giant bone has re-taken its place and Llewellyn stands beside it in stewardship with a scowling Ianto. Llewellyn has a proprietorial hand on the bone's bulbous end and there is a hat at his feet for coin. Around two cockerels stands a loose circle of men exchanging money and other things of worth. The birds leap and flurry and clash at hip-height and return to the ground with their attached spurs curved and shining. A dotted galaxy of blood on one man's gaiter. Blackened men pass exhausted from shifts and if they have energy enough to observe all this activity it is with a specie of resentment. Sleep makes demands on them. It insists. And from barrels various types of grog are ladled into beakers and bowls and even just cupped hands or gaping mouths. Poorly whittled utensils arrayed on holed rugs. The door to the puteindy remains wedged open and Mari stands at it to both greet and fare-thee-well the men who enter and leave and nearby Dic Bach begrimed from scalp to sole is drawn to a flatbed cart on which a frock-coated and tri-corner hatted man stands loudly declaiming in an accent from de Lloegr somewhere as he brandishes a small phial of urinous fluid. A score or so of such containers arrayed in a crate at his spatted and buckled feet.

- Wind from the fundament this man is saying. - Gaseous emissions from the bowel. Had a crone yesterday in the port farting the very Devil's breath I tell you and one sip of my elixir, just the one mark you, and. He sniffs theatrically with his nostrils to the sky. - Floral they were. I tell no lie. The merest ingestion of this my potion and the waft of blooms on a summer's day didst billow from beneath her petticoat. Had I the wit to think on it I could have bottled the aroma its very self and sold it off as a fancy perfume for best.

Dic Bach and the others look up at this man elevated on the cart as he is. The smile in Dic's grime.

- Or last month the man goes on. - Approached by a cove I was. Sturdy type. Stout and strong but afflicted with the tragic and age-old problem of my gender. He holds up a rigid forefinger which slowly droops into flaccidity. - You know to which I refer good sir do you not? We all do, my fine fellow. We all do. Tis no cause or reason for shame but a remedy for it is nonetheless to be sought if only to keep a smile on the face of the missus am I correct? And one sip of my elixir. He shakes the little bottle daintily between the tips of thumb and forefinger. - The tiniest sip, a mere drop on the tongue, and now the man makes his living hammering nails into wood. With his pizzle.

A shimmer of laughter.

- And hairlessness? Oh dear me no. See this? He removes his hat and bows his head and points to his own thick brown crop. - Like an egg I was, peeled and boiled, twelvemonth before last. Dabbed my potion on each morning for a fortnight and behold. And ask me about loose stools. Ask me. I was in Tregaron not four, five days ago and—

- Tis Tregaron I know full well about, says Dic Bach loud out of his dirty face. - Know all about your business in Tregaron I do.

- You spoke sir?

- I did and I said I know all about your doings in Tregaron. Fine unsullied Christian place as it is. Or was. Dic levers himself up onto the bed of the cart to take a place next to the hawker. His cap level with the man's breastbone and the filth of his face below the scrubbed and gleaming skin of the man's. - I was there too, he says to the crowd. - And with these my own eyes did I see this man here harried out of that town after having carnal congress publicly mark you with a pig. That's right you heard me I said pig.

Gasps are given out.

- That's not true! A damn lie. Total falsehood. Take no heed of this malicious little troll.

- And what is more I have it on unimpeachable authority that the elixir this charlatan hawks has been examined by men of science and found to consist of nothing else or more than his own spendings. Spendings I tell you. Dic makes a circle of his hand and jerks it at his groin. - For to have you fine Christian people and complete strangers to him drink his own onanistic emissions unbeknownst is how he attains satisfaction of his own deviant desires.

Uproar.

- Do not listen! yells the hawker. - Take no heed! An outright lie! Vilest slander and untruths! He would protest more but a flung mud-clump seals his mouth and a large stone hits his chest and rocks him backwards off the cart and the crowd surges around and descends upon him men and women and children all. Canes rise and fall. Fists and feet jerk and stamp and connect. The man tries to crawl away a figure of filth and swellings now but he is followed and dragged and the beating continues.

Dic Bach springs from the cart. Lands neatly and nimbly in the mud. A man with wilding eyes and a face smeared in blood not his own breaks from the rabble and raises the box of phials above his head and hurls it down. Madly stamps on the spilled bottles. He espies Dic Bach and presents his palm.

- Hold sir. Perilously close to parting for a portion I was. I owe you gratitude and a drink.

- For what?

- For alerting me to deviant quackery and the abnormality of his desires. Disgusted by the man I am. Appalled. Never heard of such depravity. Tell me sir do you hail from Tregaron? Your face is unfamiliar.

- Tregaron? Never been there in my life.

- Beg pardon? Then how…

Dic smiles and shakes his head. - Never met the man. Never laid eyes on the cunt prior to five minutes hence. Simply didn't take to his jib. All scoured and shining as he is. Was. Just didn't like the man.

The bloodied man studies Dic's face and his expression undergoes in seconds a transformation from startlement to great mirth. He throws his head back and lows with laughter and claps Dic on a shoulder.

- Oh you amuse me man. Such sport. The offer of a libation still stands, sir. Be proud to stand you a drink I would.

- And I would be pleased to accept.

They move away in the direction of the shebeen. Behind the cart the beating goes on. Naked discoloured flesh through the frenzy of kicking legs. These dark carnivals.

An empty bottle balanced on a stump in the forest. Drip, drip. The noise of the fayre small through the trunks at this distance.

- Aim low, says Samuel's man. Samuel himself observes.

- The recoil will jerk the snout of a sudden so aim below the target to compensate.

The pistol in Lloyd's grip at the end of his arm stiffly outstretched.

- A steady hand keep.

- And how low?

- Well, were I trying to hit a man's brainpan I would aim between his teats.

Lloyd closes an eye and squints along the rigidity of his arm and the gun and the air between it and the bottle. The glass of it absorbing some of the damp surrounding green. Drip drip.

- A smidge lower. Breathe out. Now compress.

A muscle in Lloyd's wrist gives a twitch and contracts and there is a spark and a sizzle and a hiss and then a concussive jump in the gun. There is a clattering from above and behind the bottle and a small fall of twigs and leaves. Samuel sighs.

- Tis not a strength of yours marksmanship Lloyd. That I can see, says Samuel.

- Nor of many men, says his man. - Not innately. Repetition

is key. Practice. I will re-load. He holds his hand out and Llewellyn passes him the pistol.

Samuel sniffs. - The balls do not come free. Six of them lost in these woods now I have counted.

Drip, drip. Faint shouting and laughter from somewhere beyond the trees. Lloyd sighs and coughs and spits.

The lofted traffic on the hilltops now. Travellers from the port with their many tongues and pigmentations and the inkings in their skins that announce origins in far places of ice and boil and scorch and freeze. Of endless knots of trees. Of places stalked by giant cats and other huge beasts of hungers and might. Muskets across shoulders and bandoliers across chests and there is all manner of raiment and headgear; pelts and feathers and wrappings of fabrics. Eyes epicanthic in faces all hue of integument. Teeth that glint gold in the silvery drizzle. Some tote bags of spices that sharpen and thicken the close air and some carry birds in cages, creatures of blaze that mimic the talk of humans and others have perched on their shoulders small simians with saucer eyes and tiny self-clinging hands. The exposed high rocks now all ringing motley and polyglot and also with the knock of hooves of the equines that transport men and their equipage, the wares for sale or barter and the material for dwellings and the provender for themselves and their beasts both. Bladders bulging with clean water. Heavy canvas in rolled cylinders. And there is Sir Herbert up on his sedan, the heft of him against the leaden sky on his dais on the shoulders of four men. One to each corner. Rocking as he is carried across a field of stones. Spillage from the goblet he clasps.

- Steady damn you! A smooth conveyance I will have. Spill

me to earth like my libation and take my cane to your crowns I will I swear I will by God. Split your scalps ear-to-ear I will and do it with a smile.

The carriers grunt and shift their burden slightly to re-settle it on their shoulders. Sweat on their faces beneath the slimy grime and hair wilting in their blinking eyes. Breathings stentorian and labouring.

- How fares ye Beynon? asks Sir Herbert and from the caravanserai behind him breaks a lean young man on a lean young pony. Trots up alongside. Pale features on this rider and something spectral in the fathom of his eyes.

- You summoned Sir Herbert?

- That I did. To enquire of your spirit.

- Ah. It sinks a little I confess.

- To be expected. Were it buoyant at such a moment there'd be a thing askew in your breast boy. A hollowness as it were. Steady I said!

He shifts a little on his platform. Takes a bottle from beneath the blanket that half-drapes him and attempts to fill his beaker yet spills more than he receives and hisses through his teeth and then hurls his receptacle to one side and sucks at the bottle instead. A figure scurries out of the ragged train and snatches up the discarded beaker and is re-absorbed in the throng.

- Thrips in my stomach there are Sir. A million thrips it feels.

- Aye at the satisfaction of your dishonour no?

Beynon does not reply. His head nods down between his steed's ears.

- Justice will take its course boy. Heslop will pay and that I can guarantee. Remember your training and remember the wrong that has been put on you and all will be well. Have faith and trust in the world's workings because to the true and the just it tips. To the deserving as I have on many an occasion witnessed. Nothing less than the natural order is behind you, boy. Have faith in it.

- And my second.

- Yes. Your second. Him too. A fine man.

- And he is where? Expected him here I did.

- Business in the settlement he has. Of certain urgency. But behind you he will be and that again I guarantee.

He yells for a runner and three boys approach at a scamper. Sir Herbert looks down at them.

- Who amongst you is familiar with Lloyd my groundsman? You? Then hie ye like a coursed hare to the settlement and instruct him to make haste to the allotted arena with all despatch. In the chapel or the shebeen you will find him at my guess. Find him you will wherever he may be. Now go! Run!

One of the boys sprints away over a ridge. Sir Herbert turns to Beynon and sighs at the splash of vomit that now matts his pony's pommel and mane.

- Oh Christ. Buck up boy. Tis time to become the man. He offers Beynon the bottle. It is refused with a headshake. An icicle of mucus from the underlip now. - Fucking steady I said! Must I repeat myself? Cah. In the midst I am of dumb dogs in the forms of men and what is new about that I ask myself. Buck up Beynon for God's sweet sakes and find your fucking stones.

They trudge onto the hill-ridge and into a hanging cloud. The rocking and clanking rank of them. Tatty cortege slurped into the mizzle.

In the chapel stands Lloyd on the plank floor directly beneath the hole in the roof and into all the workings of wood the warp and rot has now set unrelievedly sodden as it has been. A beam in the gap above has partly snapped and hangs to swing and creak like an inn sign. Lloyd sees it and shakes his head. - Never to be remedied now this. Irreparable I can tell. Hopeless it is.

- I detect a disappointment Lloyd. Preacher Evans drifts out of the shadows behind the pulpit. The open Bible on it now swole with the damp.- And a fatalism that behooves you not nor indeed any Christian man.

- Yes but no surprise pregethwr. Where is my man Llewellyn?

- At this very moment I know not. But the imbecile has found himself a toy.

- A toy?

- A play-pretty.

- Of what type?

- Some item found in the earth. The preacher hawks and spits. - Hewn in hell and placed there by clawed hands to be discovered. Don't ask me. Found it when searching for timbers in the shaft so he said.

- Yes but of what specie is it? This toy.

- Don't ask me man I said. A bone of some sort I am given to understand. Of freakish and unnatural proportion it is and of a provenance and purpose both something quite else in my view as against the common current as that may be. The talk is of giants. Of men and beasts of colossal dimensions that once did people these parts yet only the word 'beast' is appropriate. As is "pit". Devilish inventions and deceptions Lloyd to coax the minds and breasts away from the Creator as is their purpose and reason. Once more he triumphs.

Lloyd again regards the holed roof above. Water spots his face and he wipes it with a frayed sleeve.

- The man is without use. I cannot mend a roof with bone.

- Exhibiting the thing in the maes he was. Soliciting coin to touch it if you please.

- When was this?

The preacher says nothing.

- Is he there as we speak?

- Twould do no harm to ascertain would it not? Oh and Lloyd I will tell you this. That pew there. He points to a dented bench swamped with stagnant rain-water and sprouting fungus. - Tis Herbert's favoured seat when he visits. Always has been. You are aware no doubt of his piety and indeed his liking for routine. Twould be of benefit to you to get it fixed and quickly.

Preacher Evans leaves. Lloyd sighs and spits then coughs and spits again and into the church comes a panting boy in high colour. Tells Lloyd in billowing breaths that he comes at Sir Herbert's behest. Stands there breathing.

This shebeen heated and cramped. A pot of brown gruel on a table into which beakers are dipped and drank deeply from. Men begrimed from the pits and others drawn to the market and splattered with dung and streaked with limewash. A Romani clan conversing in their tongue maybe about the monkey which swings from the arm of one and is attired just like its owner in breeches and waistcoat and stiff-rimmed hat feather-adorned. Chittering with its small grey teeth. One man has a dead cockerel hanging head-down from the rope that serves him for a belt and others sport hares in the same way and piglets too and there is one with a cummerbund of large toads spreadeagled head-to-floor. The splayed flippered feet of them and the moon bellies. In a corner occurs a game of dice, three men in a squat and tossing the cubes against a wall. They part to allow egress for Samuel and his man but it is not a willing parting and the looks cast are not of welcome. The guard uses the barrel of his chest as a ram.

Samuel elbows to take a place at the makeshift bar and Catherine sees him and nods.

- Diod, Samuel?

- A question that requires no response woman at my duties as I plainly am.

- I did not specify alcohol.

- Tis coin I come for Catherine. The lawful levy which it is my appointed duty to collect.

- A moment to apportion it I need if you would afford me that further assistance. And here is a fowl for your table as requested. Given in gratitude it is. Cooked and seasoned.

She takes from beneath the bar a grease-clouded bundle and opens it to reveal something half-charred. Seared and stringy flesh and blackened bones and pathetic pointed wings once a bird.

- Roasted in butter none the less.

Samuel takes it from her and sniffs at it and nods. Regards the bosom of her. - Your spouse has a better eye for women than he does for target practice. That much I must admit.

- What?

Samuel sniffs. His man sniggers. - This afternoon then for the coin.

- I'll be here.

Catherine turns to serve.

Sulphuric burps from the hills. The guts of them unsettled by the palpitations on their stone skins and ejecting the ancient vapours stored and reeking of creatures long gone in flesh and bone and only gaseous now. The meat gone to ha'ants. To drifting wisps coiling across the crests shuddering and brief.

- Cah. Pathetic it is. Pitiable. Behold the wretch.

Sir Herbert gestures with his bottle at Beynon in a writhe in the mud with a hand to a bloodied shoulder and whining.

- Like an unpaid whore he does complain. Hark to him. A fleshwound that will shortly heal yet he squeals so. Has shit himself also if my nose tells me true. Pathetic he is. Worse-wounded I was when last I trimmed my toenails. Get up man.

Sir Herbert spits in Beynon's direction. His entourage stands in a loose circle and regards the writhing and the keening. Samuel there too impassive and eating bird-flesh from a bundle. One hand ripping meat from twig bones and raising it mechanically to his mouth.

- Few men worthy of the name I see today. And the world opening for them so yet precious few of gumption and ballocks enough to meet the challenge. Look on this example here, this beshitten babby in breeks. Where is my man Lloyd?

- At your shoulder I am. And indeed he does appear there, Lloyd does, out of the grey air. At Herbert's shoulder with his face pallid.

- Well stand to your office now for fuck's sakes man. Prove yourself. Heslop needs finishing he does and you must rise to meet the moment above the miniscule elevation achieved by Beynon here, not difficult though that may be. Take the pistol and finish Heslop. Hear him holler.

- Tis re-loaded?, asks Lloyd in a voice gone small.

- Tut tut man no. Protocol demands one ball only and no more and that you should know. Yet it makes a passable bludgeon that weapon does or find yourself a stone. And the boots you wear are nailed are they not? I could not care in what manner Heslop is finished only that he is and the execution of that deed falls to you. Your duty Lloyd. The moment to prove yourself is now. Observe I will.

Lloyd bends and takes up the dropped pistol still hot to his hand from its discharge and walks with Herbert the twenty steps to where Heslop sits with his face in his hands and the scarlet sluicing through the quivering fingers. His second black-clad and pale at his side.

Sir Herbert coughs and spits. - Now then. My man has a hole in his shoulder. Yours?

Heslop's second tugs Heslop's hands down and away from his face yet it could still be said that Heslop's face remains in his hands or much of it. The foam and the moaning from the hanging mouth and the lurch of the jaw unhinged beneath the black and tattered crater where the eye so recently was.

- Not an immediate killing-shot but still my man looks the fitter of the two, no? Your man will not survive his wound I think you agree.

The second nods and turns his back. Walks away. Heslop begins to gibber. Herbert sucks at his bottle and addresses Lloyd.

- Get to it then. I will not see the man suffer further deserving of such though the pig-fucker may be. Do your duty.

Lloyd turns the flintlock so that he grips it by the barrel like a cudgel. Opens his mouth as if to speak yet remains silent.

- What are you waiting for? For the man to recover? He suffers. Do your duty. I wager we'll see his brains in no more than three blows if with sufficient force they are delivered. I shall count. One.

Lloyd closes his eyes tight. Raises the gun high above his

head into the sky through which a big black bird passes over and throws a swooping shadow.

- I must rest Mari. I really must for I am raw and sore. Lou emerges from behind a hanging sheet with matted and glue-clotted hair and bruises rising on her neck and shoulders.

Mari offers some unguent in a pot. Men pace about impatiently and there are cast shadows on the hanging sheets as of some kind of puppet play which script consists solely of grunts and whimpers and squeals.

- This will soothe Lou.

Lou takes the pot outside. Where Sion y Gof is waiting in the drizzle.

- Sion? Surprised to see you here I am. Lou scoops goo out of the pot with her fingertips cupped and applies it to herself beneath her rucked-up skirts. - A first for you this is.

- Tis not. Many times have I brought these. He holds his palm out to show the four red berries in it. - More of the necessaries I bring and not for the first time. You are mistaken.

- Oh. I see. Lou shakes her head. - No longer Sion bach.

- No longer?

- No.

- For what reason?

- We must not use them for the purgings from hereon. Other ways we must seek now for these have brought a killing.

- My necessaries? A killing?

Lou nods. - Onto Morag aye. We used them to purge her as so often before with others but with her in the particular they drew more out of her than the life of the unborn.

- She is dead?

- She is alas, says Lou.

- All of her?

Lou looks at him. A soft voice: - Is there any other kind of deadness Sion y Gof?

Pink juice seeps from Sion's closed fist.

- Oh Sion. The blame nor burden is not on you. Truly it was not your intention and understood that is.

Sion's eyes clasp shut and his lips tighten into a thin line like a cut in a corpse and his epiglottis leaps in his throat.

- Sion. Sion. Lou puts a hand on his face. - Twas an accident and nothing but.

- Lou! Needed now you are! yells Mari from inside the hut.

- Listen to me Sion. To blame and hate yourself is unwarranted and is a seed from which nothing good will grow. Listen to me. Twas a mishap and only that.

Sion wipes his palm on his smock and leaves reddish streaks there. Creamy globules in Lou's hair like rancid tallow.

- Go I must now dear Sion. You did not force them on her nor indeed on anyone and who could have foreseen that Morag in her body would take against them so when none had previously.

- LOU!

- Go now I must. Lou kisses him on the brow. - Bachgen da. Bachgen da.

What to do Edric even mountain even wolves Catherine even Ianto anything please what must I do with it all all broken this never to be mended out of such I cannot make new or better guh-oh guh-oh I go she has gone

Bloodied and feathered the gimp scrabbles after what birds are left alive. Headless clumps in the dirt of the pit around him some with wings still twitching and the blood small-jetting from the ragged neck-holes. The bedlam of him and the clamour around him from the in-leaning crowd and his master with his greased tusks now drooping chestwards gathering money or dispensing it. The faces so bright in the lantern-light. Some dogs frantic barking. The penwan lunges and snatches up another chicken and raises it to his face and tears the head away with teeth filed to fangs and then a crate is upturned and a score or so of rats is tipped into the pit and then there is more scrabbling and rending and fever. This many-headed planet. The frenzy on the penwan now as he is poked into biting off one of his own toes which he then amongst laughter studies intently as if it never was his and then a sheep is tumbled into the pit and the roaring is raised to rock the hills roundabout.

And down to the river runs Sion with high knees and hard footfall. Each thump on the earth bringing a grunt. The pumping fists and the jaw jutted around the clenched teeth. Leaping over rut and obstacle and sending up splats of mud.

killed her killed her killed her killed her
escape escape
go go go go guh oh GO
MURDER MURDER MURDER MURDER
GO

He hisses in the river and steps slowly out into the flow feeling his way with his feet. The world should be made in such a way that the unpolluted and the small and the weak have special dispensation. Protection from the ravenings. That those born without a shield should have one supplied and gladly and not offered to the talons and the teeth. He bends and lifts from the water the fleece and takes it leaking in his arms to the bank where he hoists it to hang over a low branch and he studies it for some time then stops breathing and plucks a thing from its wet tangled curls and holds it up before and close to his eye: a tiny bone. A tiny bone curved like a rib with a thread of spine attached and he plucks more of these from the fleece and plucks too a skull little bigger than that of a rat yet he knows he has one such inside his own face but bigger. He holds it in his palm. The fontanelle gap in the cranium. The bone so fine it could be shattered with a whisper.

- Oh Iesu Grist, he says.

GO GO GO when the little people go
MURDER
MURDER

Two men fight. One jabs the other to the belly and puts an uppercut into the resultant whoofing stoop and the man falls with a warped nose. There is roaring and the movement of money through hands. Samuel accepts his winnings then holds his stomach and belches and groans. Buckles a bit at the waist and takes his head down below the roiling shoulders of the surrounding crowd.

Cold to Sion's touch are the ashes at the cave's mouth. He drags aside the tree-limb that has been utilised as a doorway of sorts and enters the cave. Calls out for Edric and receives only his own voice as an answer. Here the detritus of a vagabond life; bones nibbled and gnawed and a black-caked cooking pot. A pair of splayed boots still on the feet of Edric who lies still and supine on the packed dirt. Evidently lifeless for who but a dead man could ignore the hunchbacked mountain rat that has taken away his lips and nose? And stands on its hind legs chittering at Sion with a snout and teeth clotted and clogged?

Sion hisses and flings a stone and the rat skitters into the shadows. He stares down at the face. An open-cast mine miniaturised. Ploughed for morsels. The tiny skull falls from Sion's hand and lands like an exquisite paper sculpture in a fold of dead Edric's smock.

Go. Go. Go. All gone it is now or going for sure and you must now be too.

Lloyd elbows a passage through the teem in the maes gripping his lapels with hands on which blood has dried and scabbed and started to crack. His shirt-cuffs a drenched red and ferns of that blood taking root in the stubble on the face. Blood from wounds not his. Streaks of it brownish on his neck and through the hot crowd he moves reeking of roughness and at his emergence Llewellyn scampers behind his bone as if it could offer sanctuary.

- Face me Llewellyn for God's sakes. Like a child you be.

A man breaks from the crowd and takes Lloyd by the shoulder. Clean unto the collars and cuffs this man and with his buckles and buttons at a gleam.

- Touch it not sir. This is an item for science. Perhaps the most vital one of its kind thus far unearthed. An auroch if I am not mistaken or some beast even older and so far unknown and I am to transport it with all despatch to London.

- And you will carry it there up your arsehole. Lloyd grabs a fistful of the man's whiskers and shakes his head as a terrier will shake a rat.

- Unhand me you oaf! I will have respect! A man of science I am!

- I will see the back of your coat man. Speak privately with my man Llewellyn here I must and you will fuck off back to London.

He gives the man a mighty shove back into the crowd which gulps him. Ianto has wrapped his small arms around the bone and is regarding his father with defiance and fear.

- Mine father it is. Twas me who found it and brought it out and it is mine.

Lloyd ignores his boy. Moves around the bone and gibbet pole to which it is roped and puts his be-gored face an inch before Llewellyn's.

- Timbers.

- I searched for such Lloyd honest I did. On my stones I did. Went down the pit myself where you had me believe the timbers would be but twas empty excepting this object.

- Which you have been exacting a toll to touch have you not? I will take the monies.

Llewellyn splutters and Lloyd presses a forearm to his throat to force his head back against the gibbet's stanchion and with his free hand he rifles Llewellyn's pockets. Transfers fistfuls of coin to his own. Llew clutches the forearm in both hands and tries to squeeze a protest around the constriction on his neck. The crowd observes.

- It belongs to me father!

Lloyd ignores his son again and lifts Llew by the collar an inch above the mud and skews him arsewards to the ground and then takes a blade from his sleeve and saws at the rope that binds the bone.

- It is mine father! Found it I did!

Ianto holds onto his father's leg. Murmurs and movement amongst the crowd. Fixated is Lloyd.

- Get away from me boy.

Lloyd shakes his leg to dislodge but Ianto clings. An ear is hard cuffed.

- Fuck off to your mother!

The boy flees and Lloyd saws and the crowd gawps.

Tug-of-war between two stick-ribbed hounds over a length of flesh. They brace and snarl and slaver and the muscles cable and knot in their necks beneath the thin fur and blue skin blotched with mange.

The boy runs sobbing through the shifting forest of legs. Patched knees and gaiters grimed. He finds his mother at the gimcrack bar.

- What bothers you my boy?

She crouches before him and he burbles words through his terrible tears. She holds his head and plants a kiss on it and then stands upright.

- Kernow.

The big man swings his head to look at Catherine through eyes reddened with exhaustion and grog.

- I have a matter I must attend to. Deputise for a small while if you would.

Kernow slurs an affirmative word. Catherine leaves the shebeen. The Cornishman takes a stand behind the plank bar and sways and opens a bottle and drinks. Ianto looks up at him. Kernow winks.

Lloyd thunks the bone from his shoulder onto the deck of the cart. At the impact it gives out dust and dirt-spoors and a stink from deep within the world's dark and hollow and horrible heart. He stands in a shed empty of other people. Just a horse and a mule both occupied with hay.

- Fucking useless. Fucking useless. This entire place and every sheep-fucker in it.

Propped up against the gibbet and alone in the square sits Llewellyn in the churned and trampled mud. Dispersed and gone the crowd. One approaches. Catherine.

- You seek that cunt of a husband of yours?

- I do. He is where?

Llewellyn drops his eyes. - Roasting in hell for all I care. Get away from me woman.

Catherine coughs and spits and moves away.

It is a cauled shape that enters the puteindy with a wide-brimmed hat holding the caul in place plus a black scarf so that only the eyes can be seen and they do twinkle a little like drops of dew cobweb-caught. Some notion leaping in them. Mari looks into those eyes then nods in recognition.

- Occupied at the present is Lou. If indeed she is your pleasure tonight.

- Lou? Ah no, I thought rather this night the north-country girl. That accent you see.

Mari shakes her head. - Morag is indisposed.

- Until when?

- Until the crack of doom. You will wait for Lou?

- I have heard talk of a voiceless girl. New-come she is.

- And also indisposed. Resting she is away from here for hard-worked she has been. You will wait for Lou? Mari asks again.

The shape emits a sigh. - Well, overly familiar to me tho she may be I will for lack of other option. Haste her along if you would Mari. There is a pressing need.

Mari barks Lou's name and a reply is returned from behind a hanging sheet: - Shortly!

Mari looks to the cauled man who nods and they stand silent for a moment until a male throat yelps wordlessly from behind the sheet and one of the visiting sailors appears re-tying his breeches. The head of him shorn of hair and adorned with compass points inked into the pinkened skin. Mari gestures towards the sheet. - As you will sir.

- Ahoy! yells another seaman from against the wall by the door. His face in shadow. - Promised next I was! There is an orderly queue! Like a pit-prop I am!

- Then my friend the ecstasy of your release shall be all the greater will it not? The hooded man sidles behind the sheet where Lou is cross-legged in a blanket nest. Spent she seems and the smile she manages to muster is fragile.

- Preacher Evans. Hello.

- Hush child in Christ's name!

- Ach tis only the seamen here. They care not who you are

and in any case will be gone back to the port on the morrow or the day following.

The preacher removes his hat and hood and squats next to Lou and takes one of her hands in both of his.

- You will pray first?

- Of course. As always.

- It is not outwith the tally as I'm sure you are aware.

- Yes I am aware. Now hush and listen.

They both close their eyes and bow their heads and in a low voice the preacher speaks:

- Lord see fit in your infinite mercy to enwrap this here place in your protection and your love. Take your daughters herein and the service they do so selflessly provide in its necessity and keep them free from taint and corruption. Let not one suffer blow or foul word nor deed and let each precious hair on the heads of each precious one be safe. Strengthen this house against disease. Make of this place a fortress against the sins that do lurk without and look kindly upon the weaknesses of flesh and let it be never forgotten that it is entirely through the actions of us Your children that You do work. I ask this in your Holy Son's name. Amen.

Lou repeats the "amen" and the preacher releases her hand and she lies back supine and lifts her skirts and Evans drops his gaze from the bruises and the raggedness revealed. Unbuttons himself and well might chaos erupt now and it does: there is the blast of the puteindy's door being slammed in and men's voices at fervent bellow and Mari's yelled protestations and the sheet is torn down and away and there he is Sir Herbert, full in his thunder:

- Oho! Man of the cloth I see! Well now! And my, wasn't the good Lord less than magnanimous when designing your endowment! Were I you sir I would target my prayers and entreaties to —

Preacher Evans ups and flees past the chortling Beynon and out the door.

- See him flee! There he goes! Watch him absquatulate with his tail twixt his legs if tail he could be said to have! A rabbit scut the fellow sports. Pitiful.

He drinks from a bottle and looks down at Lou who is huddled in the mildewed corner. He addresses Mari over his shoulder.

- The noiseless one. Where is she?

- Indisposed. And denied both Lou and I earnings now you have.

- Pah. Paltry's the penny this spent wretch will earn you Mari. Hollowed out she is. Alone she toils tonight?

- That she does and she's already entertained more than a sufficiency she has. Tis high time for her rest.

- I'll decide that. And I will see the wares. Open your legs girl.

Lou pulls the blanket tighter to her throat. - Tired I am Sir Herbert.

- Unfortunate for you that must be then for myself and Beynon here are anything but. Anything but. And own this place and everything in it I do and that includes you whore and protect my prick I will and examine whatever scabbard I choose for it. Open your legs I said.

He takes Lou's left knee in his left hand and wrenches and regards.

- Cah. Like dog-chewed meat it is and yawning like the Dyfngwm pit. Rope my ankles afore I go in Beynon to facilitate my retrieval if you would.

Beynon cackles and raises a bottle of his own. One deltoid

bulges with a bloodied dressing and his moleskins cling sodden from the plunge in the river he undertook to cleanse him of filth although dark-smeared still they are at the rear. The dressed arm hangs loosely and seems attached to the shoulder in theory only and tinged greenish is the skin of his face and there is an unsurety to his carriage that is not wholly due to the imbibed drink.

- Loathe I am to dip my wick in such rancid tallow where so many many wicks have recently been. Splayed like a nag's hoof it is and equally as pustulent. Sooner split the arse of the mollieboy whose absence I also note I might add. A discount I will have Mari.

- Like shite you will Herbert Sir or no. Meet the tariff in full you will like any other customer. My house my rules. You are fortunate I am not demanding recompense.

Sir Herbert barks a laugh. - Your house you say. Your rules is it? Fucking priceless. He takes a deep drink and stands. - You and yours and everything you think you own and this whole place in its putrid entirety I keep in the lees of this bottle Mari. I will drink it and piss it out. Enough to fill the valley. Enough to drown every fucking thing in it. Make the lake move I will. He spreads his arms wide. A button pops off his waistcoat and the face of him beneath the skewed and steaming periwig is running in its powders and the craters in the nose appear to throb. To open and close like tiny mouths. He hawks and spits. - There it is Mari. Behold the initial trickle of the deluge to come. A new order is in creation and the likes of you must grow fucking gills if you are to survive in it. Beyond your imaginings it will be. Further than your dried mind could ever wander. The pregethwr there who I sent scuttling away? He took with him not only his shame but a ledger of the old ways. The old world went with him it did. Damp and dangling like his pitiable pizzle. A new ledger is being written. You have no notion of what is coming but attend to me and I will give you an inkling. Hold her Beynon.

Even weakened as he is Beynon's uninjured arm is of a sudden vice-like around Mari's neck. Holding her affixed. Sir Herbert tears his cummerbund away and with it the buckle of his breeches falls open and he descends on Lou and presses her face into the wall and he absorbs her and his spending is to the tune of a roar which swallows her screams and it is the first sound out of a god newly-born. A world-ending bellow of both satisfaction and insatiate need. A rat up on a beam looks down upon this tangle of grey flesh streaked yellow by the lantern-light. The flashing nostrils and the twitching whiskers and the deep berry eyes.

They look out at the world or the small piece of it that is available to them. Wrapped up in tandem in the one blanket they must touch at the shoulders as they watch the rain and pass a bottle between.

- And should he pass Catherine? Your Lloyd? What will you do should you see him?

She drinks.

Sion presses. - Will you confront him?

- Ach. Tis not the first time he has sent his boy fleeing with a pain in his chest. Twill not be the last either and that I can guarantee. But so pleased with his find was Ianto.

- And where might he be? Shall I seek?

- No. He'll be nursing the hurt of his loss as is his wont. Left him in the shebeen I did. I fret for him is all.

- He is a good boy.

- That he is.

- He is a kind boy.

- That he is. Dotes on you he does like a duckling and I know you return the affection. In ways diverse he is more your issue than Lloyd's I swear. She drinks and thinks then says: - Twas like eating the poison of a viper in truth.

- What was?

- Accepting Lloyd's emission. Each time for each child and all the other times when his seed did not catch. Burn inside me like acid it did. He is not a good man. Was once perhaps.

They sit in silence. The rain hisses down. Outside the vulcan no person does pass but a dog cocks a leg against a cartwheel then slinks hunched and wet-spiked out of sight.

- I would not refuse a draft of the broth Sion.

- The broth?

- The elixir. On which we did fly. The, the fungus-milk.

Sion shakes his head. - All gone it is.

- The lees too even?

Sion nods. - Yes but I will gather more. The rain will bring them forth from the soil it will by the morrow.

Catherine sucks at the bottle then hands it to Sion. His felid appears out of the dark and wet out-thereness and takes a place before the fire and raises a stiff back leg to lick. Sion makes some affectionate noises at it with his tongue against the back of his teeth.

- Christ this boredom will kill me Sion. On and on it goes. The endless fucking days. The weight and the grind. A horse on the fucking whim-drum I am and around and around I go without respite or relief or cease and it has put a fucking fever in me.

Sion looks at her. She looks out at the rain. Sion's eyes wet with other waters.

Yet another figure emerges from the heave and it is a little man no taller than the fighter even though the fighter is and stays seated on his stool. An eye swole shut to a pink slit and half a lip hanging. The sneer on his face and it mirrored by that of the little man.

- A great fatigue on you now there must be, the little man says, and a huge laughter is let loose. The little man is asked his name and at his reply of "Dic Bach" the laughter leaps yet more. Coin is exchanged. Other objects of barterable worth. The fighter takes his inflated hands out of a pail and flicks water from his fingers. The knuckles bunched and bulging like cobbles. He spits to one side and stands and puts up his fists. The little man with his head back on his neck does the same. The crowd roars and surges.

Catherine with her elbows on the workbench and Sion behind her and like beasts they fuck with the wan firelight on their pale flanks and the rain falling still outside. Bestial and frantic and abandoned. Sion's white arse pounds and shudders. Catherine bites her lip. The cat cleans its face. Frantic and abandoned and done in a grunt and Sion unmoored grounds himself on Catherine's pulsating back.

Dic Bach looks up from the churned floor. Tries to raise his head but it lolls on his neck and the legs shift and scissor around him and above him the man circles with his great fits swinging. Dic gathers himself into a spring and flops over onto his belly and then up onto all fours and coughs up something bilious and collapses again to more roars. The fighter turns his back to acknowledge the crowd with his hands clasped above his gleaming head and at that Dic is on his feet and he takes up the stool and leaps and scythes it full force into the back of the fighter's skull and the crack of it is a pit-prop snapping under a mountain's pressure and the man crumples on legs gone boneless and Dic brings the stool down into the man's face seven, eight times. Horror-headed the man lies still in the sudden hush which lasts for a brief moment and then in an abrupt tumult the little man is hoisted and back-slapped and passed around from man to man like a freakish child or doll.

Re-wrapped in the blanket the pair of them. Shawled in it together they are on the packed earth floor before the fire and only their heads protrude although half-hidden is Sion's in the tangle of Catherine's hair.

- I will meet you, he says. - At the port. And sail away we will.

- Oh Sion. I have no steerage and nor do you. What meagre coin I had has been taken by Samuel.

- I have wealth.

- You do not Sion. That I know.

- But you do not.

- What?

- Know. For look.

Sion moves all scrawny and naked and milky from beneath the blanket and over to the far wall where he takes something out of a cranny between the stones and returns to his place beneath the blanket and hands Catherine a small box.

- Lucifers Sion? You think to pay our passage with lucifers for God's sakes?

- Look inside.

She opens the box. Tips the contents onto her palm. - What on earth...

The gapped greyness of Sion's grin. - From your fleeces. Been saving them I have.

Agog is Catherine's gaze at the constellation in her palm.

- Taught me the word you did, Sion says. - Guh oh go. Read it on the wall of your shebeen I have.

- Of what do you speak Sion? Nonsensical you sound.

- We shall meet at the port and guh oh go we will.

Catherine closes her fist. - I do not know what to say. I have not the words.

- None are needed.

They regard each other. On the roofing the rain clatters. *When the little ones go. When they go and leave their bones.*

- Take gold for levies Samuel will.

- Ach shit on Samuel, says Catherine. - Sheep-fucker that he is and always has been. The Shinti or the Romani will exchange these flakes for coin. Present here they are at the moment. Been supplying their grog I have. We are wealthy Sion y Gof.

Sion nods. - I will wait for you then. At the port and together we will go. You and me and Ianto and the babby all of us as a family.

They stare at each other. Big things moving across their faces. Clatters the rain above and around them.

And it appears that a storm has torn through the shebeen. The pot of gruel has been overturned and some of it has hardened to tacky scab on the clinkers and the place is bestrewn with snoring bodies men and women and children all on the floor and tables and on the benches. Only one is awake and it is the Cornishman and he is pouring drinks freely for himself from whatever bottles are not drained dry and he is beaming about him and singing low. He winks again at the baby in the bassinet nearby who gurgles in reply. The sound of the rain suddenly expands and a breath of cold air hits Kernow's face and he looks to see Catherine standing in the open door and aghast she is. The boy Ianto scampers out of a corner and stumbles whimpering over the slumberers towards her.

A hammer. A noose-trap. A knife and a length of rope and some rags of clothing. Sion stuffs these items into his sack by the fading light of his forge watched by his cat. He hoists the sack over his shoulder and looks about him. Reaches out to his tomcat for one last touch.

- What has occurred boy? A moment I was gone and look at this. Chaos. Ruin.

Ianto silently watches as his mother folds a papoose around the complaining baby on the bed.

- Have you anything to say?

Ianto swallows. - Kernow.

Catherine nods. - Mule-foolish of me to put trust in that one. What was I thinking.

- I do not know mam.

- Twas not a question needing an answer boy. She holds the wrapped infant to her breast. - Hasten now. Take only what it would pain you to be without.

- I have nothing of that kind. Will we return?

- I know not for sure. One day perhaps. You have no keepsake or similar?

Ianto thinks then shakes his head.

- Then lightly we will travel. And look I have something to show you.

- What is it?

- You must tell no one. No one. Not even your father.

- What is it?

- Heed. Catherine takes the little box from her smock with the hand not clutching the baby and opens it with her thumb before Ianto's face. The contents wash his features in a golden glow as if a lantern or a torch is held inside. - Netted some stars for you I did.

- What...

- Tis gold my boy. Preciousness I will exchange for coin and then we will—

The crash from downstairs rattles the floorboards. Puffs up dust. As does the ensuing roar: - What in Christ's name!? The FUCK! Where are you woman? WIIIIIIIFE!

Heavy heavy footfalls blast up the stairs. Catherine drops the box and the contents spill and she holds Ianto to her and there she stands with her world clasped to her breast and marooed in a patch of slipped stars.

He climbs higher than he's ever climbed before. Scrambles up scree and clambers over boulders and hand-hauls himself up grykes and water-carved slashes in steep rock. He passes Edric's cave and at the side of his eye he sees a shape flutter out of its entrance, bat or bird, scavenger or psychopomp exiting the mountain's navel and chattering at a low buzz in the pre-dawn past his ear. He skirts the gibbet in which Huw Twp continues to deliquesce and he shields his nose and mouth with a hand against the stink. Up he climbs. Further up until when he stops and stands panting and looks behind him he can see no sign of the settlement only great scrolls of greyness and greenness unfurling to the horizon beneath immense cataracts of light and it is at this point that he takes up a fistful of thin earth and regards it intensely and raises it to his face to inhale. he coughs and expectorates and it is like a last purge from him. A drawing-out. He walks a ridge into the rising sun. Past walls made of stone and earth amassed into buttresses and past pits that gape in the rises like the pores of a colossal beast. Further gibbets up here with their assemblies of mouldering bones above puddles of wet moribundity. Flesh become filth. Bones hanging from hinges of sinew. He passes a lake scummed at its edges with silvery slicks of dead fish and beyond that he stops to study the carcasse of a deer hollowed out between the ribs and the head fixed skywards on the torn neck. The flesh rent by teeth. No reek rises from it so Sion saws a steak from an ungnawed area of flank and stashes it in his sack and trudges the day away from sunup to sunfall and he spends the dark hours bunched up against the wall of a great and crumbling stone structure in whose towers his forefathers held out in desperation against those who would rob them of all they held dear and worthy and the stones of this edifice are still scorched by a long-gone blaze and other signs of old war. Some scarification in stone he traces with his fingertips and guesses at the weapon that made it. Axe. Sword probably. A blade of metal many-folded and hammered and folded again. Strong, strong. The marks men make. Can make and do. He tries to coax flame from some gathered twigs and grasses but cannot so he eats the meat raw and shivers around himself as the night rolls and wails around him and the brief and broken sleep he does attain is repeatedly shredded by the dark's noises, the keenings and the screechings of its populace. The howls of predators returning to their prey or seeking it afresh or of the prey itself. He fears them discovering the plunder and seeking the thief with their raised manes and jaws that do drool and gleam in the moonlight like knives and he presses himself yet deeper into the old stone or tries to. Never before so keen and needy for the milky light to drag itself over the ridges. The sclera of his eyes star-bright in the lightless night. Such desolate sounds around. Such despairing rage contained. *We are going and we do not want to go. Leave us, leave us. And return to us what is ours and can never be again. I am so sorry.*

What the fayre has left. The jamboree detritus, the stuff left behind in the roiled mud. Shapes asleep in the lees of walls and under the beds of carts and there are empty bottles in heaps and bundles of diverse materials tumbling in the wind. Bolts of rag and odd boots. Barrels overturned or standing still and smouldering within. The bones of animals at one of which a cat squats and gnaws. Meat-birds hopping in the carriage-ways and scratting in ruts with talons. Employing bills as tools with which to capsize containers and snaffle the contents spilled. Deep within the earth is a grumble which sets all shuddering on the skin and lifts the winged things into the air and puts dimples and spirals and brief craters in the oily puddles. Like digestion within the world. Movement inside the awful bowels of it. It rolls and tumbles and things shimmer and shift slightly then rest again and re-still and the birds re-fall from out of the greasy mist.

- What ails you man? And what in God's gracious name is that almighty reek? Vomitous it is. Twill set me to spew myself.

Samuel groans in response and clutches his stomach in

a scrim of his own foulness next to the bone on the bed of the cart. Regarded from above by Sir Herbert hoisted aloft on his sedan like a seal on a rock. Swathed in blankets he is and has recently re-applied powders and pastes to his bulging face yet Lloyd can still see the legs and flickering carapaces in the periwig. A segmented brown thorax that appears for an instant amongst the weave to flex and throb. Lloyd looks away from this to Samuel yet his face does not uncrease itself from the scrunched appal.

Samuel whines. - Tis poison I suspect Sir Herbert. Poisoned I fear I am. Either that or ensorcelled.

- Poison is it? From what source man pray?

- The fowl given to me by his wife. Twas rotten is my guess. A quaking finger indicates Lloyd. - It tasted amiss.

- Oh did it?, says Lloyd. - And yet you ate it with gusto and nibbled the bones indeed. And that flagon of corn whisky you imbibed at the fight, did that taste amiss too?

Samuel buckles and pukes again. Is jack-knifed on the cart as a wet bubblesome quack blurts out the back of his breeches.

- Hell's teeth! Christ alive man! Must we suffer this all the way to Y Plas?

The sedan carriers shuffle nervously away from the cart like horses unbroken and skittish. Turn a full circle and when that circle is complete Sir Herbert has dabbed a kerchief with unguent and is pressing it to his nose.

- Beshitted myself I have.

- Several fucking times my nose informs me. Tis a wonder you have stuff left inside you to evacuate.

Another explosive fart.

- Pray for rain I do, says Herbert. - Swill you clean Samuel like the pig in shit you are a-wallow.

Lloyd coughs and spits. - Am I to be travel-mate Sir Herbert? To be besmeared with his ordure and the such?

- There is no alternative conveyance as you can see. Use the bone as a breakwater if you must. Or follow us on foot but left behind you will shortly be.

Sir Herbert looks on with some amusement as Lloyd arranges the bone between himself and the bubbling Samuel foetally curled. Slips in a slick of slime on his arse to a guffaw from Herbert. - At least I will not want for distraction on this journey. Such fuss man. And time presses. Pull yourself together and let us spur the ass to speed. There will be a physic for Samuel back at Y Plas and a hot bath for you both.

He thumps the floor of the sedan with his heel and the men beneath him step up their trudge. Breath leaving them heavy as it does the mule that draws the cart. Sir Herbert scratches his crotch and the air roundabout starts again to wetly glimmer. Lloyd coughs and spits one last time and leans to thwack the mule's rump with a willow-switch. Samuel whimpers and leaks. The midden of himself that is.

On the bed the baby bawls. Ianto too although at a lower pitch. Also Catherine on the floor with one eye swollen into a horizontal slit and a lower lip opened and an ankle held before her blackening and inflated. A bare and blood-stippled patch of blue scalp over her ear.

- Broken the bone in my leg he has. I cannot stand. Snapped my legbone the pig's cunt has. What am I to do? What am I to do?

- He has taken the stars mam.

- Taken everything he has. Everything Ianto boy. What am I to do?

In the chamber of the shebeen below them beneath the bare floorboards a calm has settled in a general stupefaction and every bottle has been wrung dry and licked clean and if there is one item of furniture unbroken it has been hidden from view. The Cornishman behind the bar now supine, beaten into black-out. The bits of a chair across his shallowly rising and falling chest.

Out from under the hanging cloud and into some sun-wash that opens this high moorland and displays to Sion blooms of a type and variety that he has never before seen. Spikes and curls and spread palms of such colourings pleasing and eye-bright. Smell them too can Sion and they have blushed and tinged the very air about. He climbs a crag and slumps his sack off his back and flares his arms wide as the small and pretty thing does that takes a bloom's colour onto a stone nearby and Sion looks and sees nicks of dreaminess. Marks that look like eyes. Colours found in the fantasies of his fungus-milk sometimes and in the furthest activities of the flames in his forge. Schematic shapes of a beauty he never expected to see in a thing alive. He bends and he studies and gasps and grins as the thing re-claims the air and flaps around his head and he observes its climb into the immensity above. Become a dot. Become entirely gone. He looks about. Peaks and more peaks a-glitter with schist and some quilled with the broken towers of a people long gone and others topped with the phantom circles and shadow traces of a people longer gone. The things of theirs made of the rottable, the wood and baked mud in chunks. This boy of the caves alone out here on this massive skin and this entirely new sensation on him and it is of a physical dryness in the warming of the sun a beam of it attached to him like a rescue-rope that has teased him out of the world of infected wet into which he was born and has existed within until this one moment. It is very big that he feels and how new that is. *A mountain of sorrow on me.*

- I fear he is going I do. Fear he will not last much longer. Will not see sunrise.

With gratitude the doctor accepts the glass of syrupy spirit that Herbert passes to him over the wheezing and damp-rattling mannequin of Samuel. Flat on his back on the scullery table and the sacking beneath him stinking and sodden. The doctor hurls the drink into his mouth and gulps and gasps and wipes his lips with the back of his hand.

- And supposition as to the cause?

- An envenoming of some sort at an informed guess Sir Herbert. What I am totally certain of however is that he has begun to pass his own inwards. No stools now just the very lining of his gut and that no man can recover from. There will be no improvement in his condition and he will not see daylight next.

Sir Herbert turns on his heels to Lloyd who is in a chair and flanked by uniformed men one on each side of him and both holding cudgels.

- So this it then Lloyd. A, a *bone* of some sort and a dead captain slain it seems by that whore spouse of yours in whose absence I perforce hold you the culprit.

- If she—

- With his last words he blamed her Lloyd as you did hear. Gift of a fowl he did declare in lieu of a payment and who can guess at what pre-meditated and maliciously-minded pollutants he ingested along with the meat. Tis murder Lloyd plain and simple. You have killed my captain.

- Entirely outwith my knowledge did my wife poison your man if indeed she did. Saw him imbibe a lake of corn spirit I did with these my own eyes. Pure rotgut which the body can process in small quantities only as I am sure the good physician here can attest. Warn him I did but the taste was on him twas clear to see and my wife's name on his lips was nothing but deflection.

- And you're certain of this how?

- Because I saw what he drank. And I know my spouse.

- Pah. Daughters of Eve and no man can ever be fully cognisant of the wiles and wickedness of their kind. Sir Herbert starts to count items off on his fingers: - One, you have failed to control your woman. Two, you have failed to curtail the excesses of my captain of which you must surely have been aware and of which office I trusted you implicit, and three you have failed to repair the chapel roof. And four—

- I finished off Heslop did I not? Whilst your man Beynon trembled like a chicken on a chopping block. Did I not do –

- And FOUR! *FOUR* and most egregious of all, where are my fucking taxes? The money Samuel was tasked to collect and some of which was to be gleaned from your whore wife. Where is my fucking money Lloyd?

Lloyd sniffs. - He wagered and lost much of it on the fisticuffs sir. The boxing.

A snigger from one of the guards. The doctor moves around the table and pours himself another drink.

- So there we have another indulgence in which you colluded. Christ alive I swear never has a man so severely misplaced his trust as I have in you. And this after I in my generosity allowed you privy to my grandest plans. Let myself down I have. I feel shame and I will have recompense and satisfaction from some quarter Lloyd and it shall be from you filled with guilt as you are. Put you to work I will. Take his garments and rifle his pockets.

The two guards fall on Lloyd and stretch him between them as if on a rack. The pallid and protuberant ribs of him bared and then too the long and scrawny thighs of him and small coins rattle to the floor as does a box of lucifers and his breeches are peeled away.

- Hold. Sir Herbert raises a palm. - The box there. Hand it to me.

One of the guards does. The other keeps Lloyd pressed to the floor in a sitting position with the cudgel held to his crown. Lloyd looks out and up through cables of hair with his hands shielding his genitals to conceal and protect. The doctor sips at his drink and observes.

- My Christ. The illumination on Sir Herbert's face as he peers into the box. His gilted skin. - So this is it. You and your spouse conspire to poison my captain and steal my tax monies and purchase gemstones. With which to do what? Tis no wonder you lacked enthusiasm at my divulged plans. Tis all clear to me now. How naive I was to trust a weasel such as you. My God. My God.

- You misspeak Sir Herbert.

- Do I by God? Pray tell me how.

- The, the mineral comes from the river. Spoil from the mine. Been panning for it I have and hoarding it in anticipation of some venture needing capital which came to me with your schemes. Tis my intent to buy myself in. To procure a wheel of my own. And the bone, it is of value too. Men of science hunger for such items they do and will pay good prices. Indeed there was one such in the settlement straight up from London expressing that very wish. Up from London he was as I say.

Sir Herbert laughs. - Oh Lloyd. Oh Lloyd. A clown you are. How could I not see it until now?

A chatter comes from the table. A mucoid rattle. Samuel's heels batter the wood briefly and then there is one final flatulent nattering. The doctor bends and presses two fingers to Samuel's neck and puts an ear to his chest and then returns to the upright.

- Gone now he is Sir Herbert. The vitality has entirely left him.

- So be it. Sir Herbert dandles the tip of his finger in the little box and toys with the preciousness therein. A yellow light comes bouncing back off his teeth. - So the world of the living no longer has a place for my captain then I no longer have use for you Lloyd. Just so. Tis trouble you are. You and that spouse, wretched and murderous. Learn from my mistakes I will as we all must yet so piteously few do and that is why I am I and you are you. Look at you I would tho it nauseates me so to do. Your pizzle and ballocks on the cold stone of my scullery floor. A plenitude there is of men to replace you and worthier and no I care not for your bone nor indeed you. To me you are a biting flea. More bother than you are worth. I have this do I not?

He rattles the matchbox next to his ear. - Time it is for us to part now Lloyd. For our business relationship such as it was to be terminated. I will see you swing a mallet and wield a shovel and in chains I will see you and if this is true about the mountain stream giving up gold then a militia I will despatch there to pan every fucking thimbleful of the water that I will move. Gut and level the mountain entire I will. Extract every last precious fleck from it that it is possible to take. Your wife and every other useless cunt of a sow must learn to sprout fins and gills. Into the garden with him.

The guards haul Lloyd across the kitchen flags. Lloyd bellows. The doctor drinks and looks on as Samuel starts quietly to rot.

Close enough to the surface to be half-in darkness and half-in daylight the Yorkshireman hacks with his pick at the walls of the shaft and dislodges flitches of rock which Kernow with a rabbit's scut affixed to the breast of his jerkin bends and buckets. Above them and thrown in its angles against the grey sky cranes the engine known as the Miner's Friend. It chugs and clanks and vibrates its pumping-pipe between the two men and the rattling thrum and mutter of it fills the shaft. Makes of it a sunken tube of sound. The pick is swung and swung again and more boulders are bucketed. The men huff and grunt knee-deep in wobbling water. An abrupt concussion blooms above and sparks descend in a flaming hail and instantly the water level begins to rise and the two men scramble for the knotted rope with tiny fires in their hair. Knees and thighs and hips submerged. Bellies and then breastbones that rapid. Pick flung and bucket dropped and the men scrat and scramble for the rope and against the flowstone walls of the shaft and the now limp pumping-pipe itself as they seek holds for toe and for finger. Collarbones submerged. Throats. Nails ripped from fingertips. Yell and bellow and scream and scrabble. Kernow attempts to clamber up onto his workmate's shoulders and both of them then crumple beneath the lifting water black and oily and for a brief time a-boil with the frantic bubbles of their last breaths. The water comes and comes.

Anklechained to a ploughshare Lloyd swings the mattock into the bone. To pound and to pulverise. Samuel has been interred in the cabbage patch also by Lloyd and there is now a great fatigue in his muscles and that and the weight of his shackle might have added years to his carriage and he shuffles about the garden like a much older man. The two militiamen stand nearby and observe and Swinburne is seated sketching on a stool. Lloyd mixes the clinkers and grit of the bashed bone with manure and digs it into the compost heap that steams in the evening sun. He turns the mulch over with his shovel. The ploughblade scrapes and screeches across the cobbles. Lloyd releases the shovel and regards his blistered hands and drops slowly into a squat. Looks over at Swinburne.

- Must you compound my shame man? Is this fucking necessary?

No response.

- Vexatious enough as this punishment is tis made far worse by being used as the subject of a, a fucking rendering. To be walled in Herbert's office no doubt. Fuel for his gloat and glee. I suffer as it is without my likeness being the object of that man's gawp. Tis a freak you are making of me.

Still no response. The militiamen are now conversing amongst themselves by the herb garden in the fumes of rosemary and bay and Swinburne is sweeping charcoal across his page.

- I exist Swinburne. Still I exist. Why this frozen tongue?

Swinburne does not look up. Does not even still the movements of his hand. But speaks: - Forbidden I am to converse with you Lloyd. Which in itself is too much to utter.

- A low tone keep then. Herbert's hearing is not that of a wolf's. A low tone we can keep. Do I not exist yet?

But Swinburne has returned into his willed silence. Nothing

but focus on the marks he makes. Lloyd importunes twice more but receives only silence both.

- Well fuck you then. Stuff your mouth with the gleet of sheep. Lickspittle to a cockalorum as you are. As you have ever been. The shame is piled on me with injustice but burn in your breast it should. Sooner be me than the drizzling turd of yourself even in this scenario. Soul I have kept.

Lloyd drags his burden to the rhododendron bush beneath which he lies and curls up like a cat in a sunbeam only utterly without the contentment. And the darkness comes down and Swinburne and the guards withdraw into the house and this is how Lloyd will spend his final days, dragging his weight around the garden and feeding on the scraps thrown to him out of the scullery window or picking for morsels in the compost heap and sleeping beneath the nodding calyxes and leaves through rain and hail and frost. Soon the abrasions of the steel anklet will invite gangrene into his flesh and he will fester whilst alive until the toxins take over his blood entirely and he will die supine on the gravel path one morning with the smell of rosemary and his own necrosis in his nostrils and he will be interred by the newly hired factotum in the brassica patch within touching distance of what was once Samuel.

Once he cut out the figure of a man on horseback from stiff cloth and held it anterior to the glow of his forge and made it canter in silhouette for the delight of the watching Ianto and now Sion sees that figure again on the ridge. The nodding head of the steed and the erect back of the rider. He watches it traverse the ridge silently and vanish behind a huge thumb of rock wheeled about by big birds and then he moves on again. Away from that ridge and towards the sea. Thinks he can smell the salt and vapour that he has been told it emanates but knows that it is likely just his fancy so far inland as he is still. He crests a hill and comes across a lake on the rushy shores of which some cowled figures sit around a small fire. He greets them but only one looks up at him with one eye faded blue and the other turned to milk in a tangle of white hair within the conical brown hood. Sion recalls Edric's tales of the Afanc and also of other beings gone from the world. That tiny skull. The bits of Edric's own skull glimpsed through the rat-ravaged face.

When the bruises on her face have faded to yellow and her wounds have closed into cicatrice and with her ankle still splinted between two cabled boards Catherine knocks at the door of the bordello and calls Mari's name. The door opens.

- Catherine.

- I hear you have lost a girl.

Mari says nothing.

- And I have lost all Mari. Everything. Tis all gone.

Mari coughs and spits. - I have lost all girls Catherine. My workforce entire. My mollieboy too. Taken their pox-ridden hides they have over to Ffair Rhos in the hopes of a cure from the abbey waters. In vain in my view for gave off a reek they did all of them and nothing that smells that way will long be sucking air. Parts of my poor Lou even fell out they did.

A wind blows through the settlement. A great gritty breath from the warrened mountain and its stipplings of spoil. Ripples the stagnant fluids in the wheelruts and dusts meniscus and mud with thin white powder like chalk.

- I can bring in coin Mari. Hungry we are. My childer waste. Another ship is to berth shortly I am told and I need to eat and make for the port. My children they fade and waste. Any urge I will satisfy.

Mari's lips turn pale. She indicates the bulge of Catherine's belly. - Some men there are who favour those in your state and who are far gone in gravidity as you are but such men hold a rare preference Catherine. You will want for the paying customer regular until the birth is done and you have regained your form. That I can guarantee you.

Catherine's face crumples and she drops it into her hands. Mari puts one palm on Catherine's bent back and the other to her own throat.

- Oh sweetheart. Oh poor woman. Oh Catherine.

On these high moors do the meat-birds mantle blackly over their prey. Wings akimbo like capes and their blood-brindled breasts out-thrust like the prows of ships. In tall grasses the chicks of one such avian in an invisible cloud of ammoniac choke and fleshrot spread their stubby and tufted wings at Sion and open their beaks to hiss. The coals of their eyes. Three of them in a line in perfect imitation each to the other and *so brave you infant demons. Fear me never I carry no ill-will and how could there be room for such when my wanting to be you fills it all everywhere? Accident, twas. To harm in any way was not my intention or mark no not even scratch the skin. So sorry I am.*

He moves on. Ever closer to the sea. Down a great gouge in the earth along which ice once chased humans and some of the stones in that gully bear indentations in the marks of the weight of fleeing feet when rock was soft. Depositions of peat prior to solidification. Another night comes down and Sion at a weary distance circles a wide splat of bogland across which pale blue flames flicker and drift the colour of cornflowers and starlight. Heatless fires released from the bursts of quag bubbles to shimmer and waft and flicker away and Sion knows that they are to be respected and avoided and that they are of a specie with the things seen within the mineshafts that populate the tales of those who labour in their underworld, the side-eye shapes and forms. Intruders uninvited and unwanted and departed from the bodily. Do not stay long with them. Do not bide. Spirits absconded from their places of punishment and no good can such carry. To escape from the pits vengeful and bitter and there to lure into sucking morass or over a sheerness or into the border-less places of their own endless panic and pain. Do not stay long with them. Do not bide. And that the stars have talons Sion knows that too and can see the proof. And that the wolves and felids hereabouts have teeth.

And then another light in the darkness, in the middle distance with curls and colour known to Sion's eye. The reddish jumping ferns. Faint voices. Cold and hungry he is and made careless by that and so he is drawn. Warmth of that fire and the possible heating of victuals despite the potential depredations of brigandage and the taking from Sion of what very little he has but the gape in his belly and the frost in his bones are very loud.

They squat in blankets and shawls around a fire across which a carcasse is spitted. The smell makes Sion wildly emboldened and he joins the group without invitation or even salutation and all heads swing at him and he sees their faces in the flamelight and the unfamiliar pigment of the skin almost copperish. The hue of peaty shallows. They speak at him in an alien tongue and he looks at each to the other in climbing fever but one then addresses him in the Saesneg and asks him who he is and what might his mission be. Angled scars on this man's face and three ribs of a tiny creature punctured through one earlobe. The man and Sion talk and offer to each other what needs to be offered and after a time Sion is handed a chunk of spitting and oily flesh on a dockleaf which he immediately thrusts into his face. He is told that these people have fled here from a faraway land to escape the rapine of a flood of devils like them but not like them and some of whom may even have their origins in these hills hereabouts but whose souls underwent some awful mutation during the crossing of the large waters. They show him tchotchkes and trinkets some in diminutive likenesses of men and beasts and they show him necklaces of pointed teeth. Polished amulets once endowed with the powers to resist horror and harm yet not long since proven ineffective. Sion asks them about grymalkin's huge and cow-sized brocks and then about bison at which word there is a wail far off in the outer dark and the man with the face the likes of which Sion has never seen tells him of men that wear their true skins on the inside and of wolves and other raveners that walk upright and are driven across the earth by nothing other than insatiability. Sion is told that the wolves cry because they can see the end of themselves and that we live amongst things that one day we will not and that a future will be utterly without except for the memories of such which too will recede but we must live and behave as if this will never come to pass because to not do so is to suffer. To beckon many and various wounds. And why would we do that when the world will impose a plenitude of injury as it has ever done even when the sun was just a hole made by a nail in oilskin. Even before the dirt writhed first into man-shapes and took to its feet. New devils have come. New devils have been born. Seek new weapons against them we must for they will not cease to gnash until everything that we have ever valued has been transmuted by them into turd. Soon the final bison will die.

Digesting meat and invited to do so Sion lies back amongst these people a few of whom are sleeping already and he is draped with a blanket that smells of dog yet no such animal is apparent. The fire tuts and snaps at the fine drizzle. Sion senses sleep nearing like a fogbank and he asks of the face-scarred man what he and his kind will do now in this land and he is told that work underground will be sought. *I do not know for the surety,* says the man. *We have been driven to walk up and down on the earth.* Sion studies this man's face in the firelight and through the needles of soft rain and would reach out to it but slumber takes him and when he awakes he is alone on the moor and the fire is a clump of smouldering ashes latticed with charred and nibbled bones. Tiny spouts of grey powder being lifted by the wind.

The militia appear overnight without alarum like predators sent by the moon. Liveried in blue gaberdine and all armed with cudgels and some also with firearms. They take over the shebeen and sequester some dwellings as billets and the maes fills up with the freshly evicted and one man who will not surrender his hovel is overpowered and hung from a tree-limb then cut down and propped up blackfaced and tongue-bulging on the bed of a tumbril and situated in the square as caution. One militiaman with some silvering on his epaulettes positions himself on the cart too and speechifies with much indication of the dead man. Much gesticulation to his lifelessness. *Who would join him. Who amongst you.* At a point in the mid-afternoon some gunshots are heard and by dusk there is a new outline against the sky up on the ridge that banks one end of the top lake — the raftered legs of a tall machine. By dawn that machine has evolved and has sprouted a tube and a repeatedly nodding fulcrum and the legs of another structure have appeared alongside. Faces in the settlement stare up. Eyes twitch to follow the lever that bows and bows.

They stop the hooded man on the mule at the outskirts of the settlement on the track that circles the Dyfngwm barrow and leads into the interior. Three of them with bludgeons brandished. They order a halt and an unveiling.

- Show yourself. Reveal your face.

The rider does. The militiamen snort.

- A preacher. And where might you be bound?

The pregethwr leans and spits. - Away from here. Far away from here.

- Aye but to what destination? Which chapel in particular is it now whose desolate and needy flock will benefit from your benedictions?

The speaker grins wide. Dark shards of food caught in his teeth. Yellowed incisors like fangs.

Preacher Evans rubs the bulb of his nose with a sleeve-cuff. Grey curls stuck to his skull. Evident that his preference is to not look directly at his inquisitors but his eyes are drawn and drawn again.

- Any one of a great many. The need is widespread. Extensive it is.

- Which is no answer to my query but no matter. Yet you leave this place why? Think you not that the souls in this settlement require guidance in spiritual issues at this moment more than ever, no?

That grin. Vulpine and leering and flanked by the sniggering snouts of the men on each side.

- There will shortly be none remaining. Preparing to flee they all are without exception. Imminent an exodus is and is that not what your master demands? To avoid the weight on his conscience of the drowned, poltroon that he is? And if conscience he harbours which I do doubt. Preacher Evans swallows. Swallows more words.

Now the grin goes. - Advise you I would to avoid such smears. Slander and calumny I *will* beat on regardless of the vocaliser and his station. Man of God or shit-shark I care not. Any head that sullies the name of Sir Herbert I will break and happily. One warning you are permitted and that has now been given.

The mule nods to crop and the preacher tugs at the reins. Small as the beast is the preacher's mud-caked shoes dangle a mere inch above the earth.

- Foretell this day I did.

- And what day might that be pregethwr?

- This day. This very day. The day of the arrival of such as yourself and the final breaching of the dam.

The militiaman's gaze flicks up to the machines on the ridge and the preacher releases an exhausted sigh.

- I speak in metaphor man.

- Which word I know not, says the militiaman. - Speak plain. Uneducated wretch that I am, agreed?

Evans shakes his head. Recognises the coil in the militiaman in the cords of his neck and in the knuckles on his bludgeon. Even somehow in the abrupt thickening of the drizzle.

- We need not converse any further, says Evans. - You are about your task and I am about mine and my passage is a free one still. Both of us are subjects of a higher edict are we not? In the sight of Christ I will be on my way.

The militiaman licks his teeth. His partners regard him and

look for a signal and when he eventually nods and takes a step backwards they do the same. He gestures with his club.

- Proceed then. Be on. For what use would a whoremonger have of this place now that all the whores have gone? Taken by the pox hah? You'll be scratching at your prick and stones within the hour.

Evans conceals his face in his hood. Flicks the reins and kicks his heels into the mule's ribs.

- A whoring man of God, the militiaman says. - We have your secrets clear and stink they do. Think we are here with corruption in intent? Be fucked man we are here to cleanse. To purify. To open the way for a God purer than the one you beseech. Be on and take your taint of rotting sin elsewhere.

They watch the preacher shrink in size. Moving away rocking on his steed. When he rounds a hump and can no longer be seen all three of them in unison hawk and expectorate into the mud.

Not even in dream no. Nor in the fantasies of fungus has this been seen, this vastness and blueness and glitter. The sparks off it only seen ever in the precious pellets picked from Catherine's fleece when dragged out of the stream. Ships on it gradually shrinking the closer they get to the horizon and Sion has seen their likenesses on the pictures in the shebeen that solicited for steerage. The heart of him swells. The head of him swells. Assailed by possibility he is. How blue it is below him and how green in both so many shades. What things from magic could live within with fins and scales and tusks and of colours unknown and too what lands across it. What other worlds. Unpassable it seems and must surely be yet he knows people who have done just that. Met some of them yesterday indeed who warned of the wolves within. Ate and slept alongside them he did. Gave him meat they did and safety. This is the sea. Here it is below him. This is the sea. All the stories he's heard.

Sion descends the hill. Over a swell of tufted rock and then he sees the port below him and the mast-forest of its harbour. Rooves and steeples all drawn together of slate and thatch and canvas and thin hammered metal. Smells, as he nears, to which his brain searches for nomenclature yet of past experience and contact there is none. Still they tickle his nose and flood his mouth with spittle. Onions he knows and fish-stink. Oil and grease and smoke. But there are many others that sprint and gambol in his face to which he can apply only one word that he has heard many times on the lips of sailors passing through the settlement and that one word is *spice*. Big white birds turn circles above the roofscape and cry like children in dismay.

He goes down. Steps onto a track of packed earth then leaps backwards off it again as a man on horseback blatters past. Bellows some words at him through his trailing dust-smudge. Beyond the track are the close-packed backs of hovels and at the casement of one is a watching woman from whom Sion's wave receives only a scowl in return.

This is the port. Place of new lives and of tongues and skins unfamiliar. Sion enters it as his cat would enter a place of noise newly returned to silence, his tattered boots paw-deft and paw-soft on the cobbles and hard dirt and with his face a-hum with alertness. Vigilance razor-whetted. He turns a corner and is snatch-gulped by a mass of sudden motion and there are skins the colour of coal and skins the colour of toad-belly and skins the colour of curd and skins the colour of soil and skins the colour of ale. Of cheese-rind. Of cox-comb. There are shouts and greetings and curses in tongues that sound to Sion like sounds no human throat could ever make. Faces press at him. Hands reach. Heads in shawls and wrapped bulgings of cloth. Heads shaven and inked, one with a huge staring eye on the top of the skull forever looking to heaven. Metal glints in the flesh of faces. Metal forms hands stiff from cuffs as does wood also and some lower legs have been reconstructed from darker wood and some from whalebone, one with the teeth peaking up the shin like the stem of a rose towards the codpiece made from reddish pelt. Agog Sion is. His bounding senses. Hands thrust things at him, raw meat and dead fish and strips of hide. Coin is solicited. Contraptions of metal and wood. Knives like both hoofpicks and sabres. Flintlocks and shoes and things that steam in clouded paper. It overwhelms. Sion whirls and shudders and escapes into a shebeen where on the beam that serves a bar is a tiny child covered sole to scalp in thick greenish fur. A tasselled cap on its head and a fancy waistcoat of brocade. It bears and chitters its tiny teeth at Sion. Screeches.

- Hoy now! Whisht! A large man pops up from behind the beam and scoops the child up and puts it to perch on his shoulder where it wraps its tiny arms tightly around his head and puts its juddering eyes on Sion. - Tis no way to greet a new customer Edward. A welcome tavern we keep. Heed not my monkey, friend. Merely excitable is he. Tis just the nature of his kind.

- He is a monk?

- A monk? Add on an "e" and you will hit your mark. What is known as a "monkey" is this fellow here and he has been my close companion for quite some time. There to greet him straight off the boat I was. And you. Fresh arrived in the port?

Sion nods. Staring at the creature.

- From where?

- Dros y mynydd.

- Saesneg if you please. The tongue of the interior holds no reference for me.

- Over the mountain I have come.

- And you are here for what? Work, passage? Pure leisure?

Sion sees the creature's fingernails. The red thread it sports around its neck.

- What is it? asks the man again.

- Pardon?

- Your purpose boy. What is it that has called you to the port?

- A woman.

- Ah a woman. Like so many before. Well you must narrow your options and prioritise your wants lest you lose yourself in the variety available herein. What sort of woman, in the specifics?

- She is called Catherine and she will come with her childer and we will go.

Both the man and his little familiar slit their eyes at Sion. - Now there's a particularity of detail the likes of which I've never hitherto encountered.

- I wait for her and she will come.

The man scratches at his ear and the creature grabs his finger in both its hands and clings. - If you say so boy. And while you wait for this Catherine tell me which libation you will partake of.

- Pardon?

- What would you like to drink, man?

But the barman is speaking to a departing back. Sion has left and re-joined the outside crowd in the brightness unexperienced that brings the lids of his eyes together and puts a heat on his head. Bashed about he is by the passing surge and spun out onto the track and back again by the gritty wash of a cart yanked rattling past by two heavy horses and stacked with bales of branches. Spins does Sion. Battered by a babble and whirled. A small dog snaps at his ankles. From a window above him some waste is thrown and he must skip backwards to evade its foul fall and splatter. In this place are babies born all green-furred about and which communicate through chatterings and shrieks.

He finds himself at the waterside. The harbour. So tall the masts and so many and the hulls swelling above him bigger than any building he's ever known and hitched by ropes as thick as his waist to the raucous rocks of the sea-walls that gleam greenly thick and somehow meatish. He feels hands squirming into his pocket and he slaps them away and presses his back to a slimed wall and watches a man tip things into a boiling pot, things that clitter and scramble with claws and whiskers and stalked eyes. Grotesque spiders straight from fever and with warty and knobbled armour and with blades and axes grown from their own external bones. A cart passes him and on it is a fish larger than two men laid end-to-end and with a mouth crammed with blades. On hawsers objects sway through the air above him, boxes and items of furniture and machinery in great blocky arcs through the sky. Such noise and what a marvel that anyone here could understand the other. He sees golden teeth. He sees faces tattooed with pitchforks. Objects proffered to him of no shape and every shape and at each of which he shakes his head. He tries to count the various banners that adorn the masts but cannot and nor can he name their colours.

Later on that first day he will hide and bed down in a dockside shack. Poor hutment built from packing crates and sacking probably by sea-gypsies of some sort. He will lie hazily vigilant for their return and kept from deep sleep also by the sounds and activity from without, the cries and calls from throats and the groans and squeals of simple machinery. Windlasses and winches. In the grasped snatches of his slumber he will dream of small skulls. Small skulls disembodied and suspended in a darkness which are of a sudden sucked back into the blurred faces behind them, three faces of scumbled features and three different sizes — that of a woman and a boy and an infant.

For some days he survives on whatever scraps he can scavenge from the boxes of fish and vegetables on the quay and when such pickings are unavailable he eats sea-cabbage and dulse and laver from the rockpools and on whatever pabulum he can take from the rocks and sand, flesh that lives in razored shells or that clings to rocks. The occasional armed spider that he must break open with a stone. At times he begs and in facilitation of that he learns shards of various tongues, some from other lands and also those indigent to his own or at least this littoral part of it — cant and mumpers and parlay and pidjin and Shelta. His mouth whirls and dances and the powering mind behind it often storms. He waits. He waits with the large humpbacked rats and the canny cats that hunt them in hovel and hideaway and there are others like him who he learns to avoid. He watches the sea and sends his soul over it. Emits frequently a piece of himself to a land far away. To whatever shores may await. When the short cold days and long icy nights come he contracts an illness severe enough to put a whisper on the back of his neck and he is forced to solicit succour from the smithy in the back streets of the port who gives him a nest of blankets next to the fire and coaxes him out of his delirium on fish-head soup and oatcakes that rip his throat. With the return of his strength he repays the vulcan with assistance in his toil and his aptitude for the work is quickly assessed and appreciated to the extent that the vulcan's absences from the forge become more and more frequent until one day Sion realizes that he hasn't seen the man from full moon to full moon without any deleterious effect on his commissions so he comes to be seen in the port less as the smith's assistant and more as the smith. Horseshoes they want. Hasps and hinges and buckles and blades. Chains and locks and boots to be hobnailed. Spikes of all sizes. Spring-traps large enough to catch a man. Snows come and go. When not working Sion drinks and thinks of a woman wailing lost and alone on the dank upness of the moors or become bones in the lee of a fin of rock or gulped by the quags so that only a reaching hand can be seen. He drinks and thinks of children eaten by wolves or by wolves in the shape of men. He thinks of skulking nameless beasts. He dreams of spinning in an endless emptiness. He puts coin aside and with it purchases a slice of land on the clifftop on which to build a Ty Nos and this he does one summer's night when with the first star he digs a footing and with the red rise of the sun he is sitting within four lopsided walls and a crooked roof with a kettle boiling on a hearth. Men appear to proclaim the dwelling lawfully his and he makes a mark on a page at their behest and when they leave he stands on the bluff on which he has built his home and sees the iron filings on the horizon grow into ships as they near the land. He will spend a lot of time watching this happen. He sleeps half of that first day away and wakes in a panic. Within him he will carry an almost palpable air of loss and distraction which he banishes with the endless whack of his hammer when working and with alcohol when not; two short men periodically appear from the hinterland to sell him ewers of their own brew and

Sion becomes a reliable customer. Concocted from roots and leaves. Honey and flowers. All of it fiery urinous. And too Sion becomes a known presence in the taverns and shebeens of the port so much so that the little furred mannikins cease to chitter and whoop and show their teeth at his appearance and the big colourful birds cease to shriek. On one occasion at that time of the year when the fast forktailed birds re-appear Sion has a memory of a large and comforting hand so he boils up some fungal broth one morning and drinks it but it transports him not to a place of wonder but of mighty regret during which he sits alone on a rock high above the sea and weeps with such force that he fears for the eyes in his head and he does this until the sun has been drawn back below the waters so he never makes the elixir again. He acquires a woman and her child who turn his hovel into a cramped and loud box so he equips the forge in the port with some items of furniture and it is there that he can nearly always be found and indeed it is where he is one night teasing heated metal ingots into nails when he hears through the greasy sea-fog that has claimed the port a spirit somewhere in it wailing his name.

The walls still ring with the roaring and the sheets they drip drip onto the floorboards. From without is the never-halting kuh-*thump* of the nodding engines on the ridge and within there is the exhausted sobbing of Catherine and the mewling of the wetly caked infant and the faint whutter of the candles. Such a scene that these hilltops have seen. Time and time over. Soft words from Mari:

- Well done. Oh well done cariad.

Bloodied towels in twists roundabout and a bowl of pink-swirled water as if in this simple room a deer has been butchered. The blue-black tendril of the umbilicus still linking the newborn to the mother.

- A new life Catherine. Another beating heart.

- Which is why I weep, Mari.

Mari strokes Catherine's matted head and bends and bites the umbilicus through and ties it off and catches the slobber of the afterbirth in her cupped hands and takes the steam and ferric fumes of it to the window and lets it slide away. Outside it splats nearby to the militiaman who looks up at the casement with little interest and then down again with more at the dog that has already started to snuffle.

- What shall I do Mari? What am I to do? Three bellies I have now to feed excluding mine own and no means have I to do so. Lost I am. Further adrift and hopeless I am now than even yester eve I was.

Mari stares. Sees in the candlelight Catherine bow her head to the tiny and streaked and trembling baby she is holding to her breast and how all trauma is held in that form. In the tiny purple foot. The toes already flexing. Shadows cast across like the phantoms or promises of the meat-birds been or to come absconding with carrion or in future search of the same.

Dic Bach enters the room. Stands bouncing on his feet at the side of the bed.

- There is space in my stable for you Catherine and I—

- You will fuck off out of it Little Dic spits Mari. Properly spits; a clotted gobbet from her lips. - Importunate as you are even shattered as she still is. Have respect man. Rein in your appetites.

She wrestles him towards the door and pushes him through and out and no sooner is the door closed is it opened again and Llewellyn advances towards the bed to stand there keen and eager.

- Christ Llewellyn! You fucking men! Allow the woman time to recuperate would you ever fucking not? Given birth she just has! Out of it!

Full head and shoulders taller than Dic Bach as Llewellyn is he must be arrointed with a blade which Mari brandishes swiftly and with the glinting point of it drives him back through the door. Which she slams and leans against. Wash of flamelight momentarily across her face. Catherine's head still pressed to her newborn and a thin wind blowing at the mullioned window and beneath the crack of the door. Male voices outside and the growling of a hound and still and always the thuds from up on the ridge in the incessant rhythm like the heartbeat of a beast huge and asquat and brooding. Fomenting and overseeing all.

Water level lowering in one of the lofted lakes of the high parts. Ancient stone seen again. Peat-preserved treetops approaching petrification once more in the air. Things turned by time to what they were not. Thump-*thump*, thump-*thump*. Far away from their origins, from what they moulded molecules into what manner of existence uncountable mornings ago. As the old stones appear so the newer ones below in the valley are submerged and at this exchange the engines nod and lift and nod again and go on doing this unceasing as if in approval repeated and enthusiastic.

Catherine sleeps. Ianto sleeps. The baby sleeps. The infant sleeps and when awake utters not one sound as the gaze floats around the room searching and unfocussed and seemingly content to be that way.

The scree starts to slip. Like a giant sloughing of skin it starts to shift downwards with the new waters now within it. Stone in motion. Rock on rock as the mountain shrugs with the weight going from atop it. And such a weight. Such a weight. The spread of water where water was not and all that is not water taking on its properties. New trickles and new rivulets. New springs. Skin of stone loosening and starting to slip. Descend. A grind and a groan and soon the inevitable roar. The birds rise up and take themselves away into the grey sky. The machines bow and thump and bow and thump and put the whole mountain into slow flow.

- Why did they put him in there mam?

 - Because he'd been a bad man. Come away from him now.

 Catherine steers Ianto by the nape away from the swaying ruin of Huw Twp. The two small heads in the papoose on her back nodding loosely in sleep and not for the first time she thanks the hunger of her hollow breasts for the somnolence that results.

 - Will they put me in one of them?

 - They will not.

 - Why?

 - Because you're a good boy.

Ianto turns his head as he walks the more to regard the gibbet and its captive.

 - Do not look back bachgen da. Only ever look forward. See where you put your feet for the ground is uneven.

This little caravan up on the high parts. The smell of released water behind them as they move towards a different fluid. Peak over peak over peak and the trudge of their passage. The wind up here. What was at one time a man called Huw is spun by the wind as he hangs and rots to look after them with the picked-empty drains of his sockets.

They flee the settlement on foot and back of beast and on beast-drawn tumbril. The hastening immersion about. Cows lumber and poultry flaps away and cats and dogs bound higher. Earth squelching around boots and bare feet and amassed they are these refugees with what chattels they can strap and have strapped across their bodies and bundled on their backs. The water gulps the stones. The water gulps the walls. The sheds and the huts and the hovels. The water climbs the chapel walls in reach of the punctured roof.

His name in the sea-fret. Sion looks up with a snap as would a cat at a slamming door. Some wind there is so perhaps the sussenance of a collapsing shore-wave sharing the sibilance of his name yet again it comes and louder and it is the voice of a woman calling only his name like a spectre of yearning in the clogged and milky and salty fog. And then taking shape before him.

- How did you find me?
  - I asked, Sion.
  - Who did you ask?
  - Does that matter? Fisherman he was. Dockworker. Something. I do not rightly know. Described you to him I did. Outlined your features and told him you had some facility with metal and here he directed me. You must mean the new

vulcan he said and showed me the implements you have made for him. Spoke highly he did of you Sion y Gof.

With scabbed sections of sole and toe bared through the rags they have been shod in to either reinforce or entirely replace exhausted shoes the three children sleep. Cwtched up in the corner by the fire the three of them part-swaddled in the only blanket in Sion's possession. Fed on fish-tea and black bread they've been. Ianto supine between the two smaller each with their heads to an armpit of his and his arms around them. Deep deep under in slumber all three.

- His eyes are yours, says Catherine.

- He has them closed.

- When they are open. The same shade as yours they have. And look. The nose. That too is yours in the form. As if sculpted in clay in the image of you is he.

For quite some time the only noises are what the flames give off and the breath of the sleepers and the faint sound of labour from the harbour. And in the near distance the soft lift and drop of the sea dampened by the fog.

- Where is Lloyd? asks Sion.

- Taken away. Sir Herbert took him. Who has now flooded the settlement. I have no man and no dwelling Sion. We must go. That word if you recall. My lawful husband rots in a cell for all I care. Beat me he did like a dog.

- Alas I have no steerage. And you tell me the gold is gone.

- Yet you have work and you are earning. The ruin has arrived Sion. And there was an arrangement was there not? A promise. Here I am with my portion of it. See me.

Sion looks away from her. - Had you lost I did. Lost or dead or both. A woman and her child I now have Catherine and a Ty Nos up on top. Rooted now I am. Lost or dead or both I reasoned so long it was. You and the childer.

Catherine puts her face in her hands. Sion sees the rawness of those hands and the filth ingrained and the bared dark red bed where a nail has been ripped away.

- What must we do now? Tell me. What in God's name do we do now Sion? Stayed in the settlement I should have and drowned. Trusted you I did. And our arrangement. Ruin. All is ruin.

Sion again looks away from her. He looks at the children. He looks at the flames and his tools arrayed about and his commissioned projects part-completed: the hubs and spokes of cartwheels and the braces and buckles up on the walls on hooks. Concentric hoops of barrel brackets stacked one on top of the other to the height of the hearth's lintel.

- Tell me what to do Sion. I have your child. Your issue. Here I have come with three childer across the mountain and to what but abandonment. Made a promise you did. An arrangement we had. You cannot abandon our baby. Had you various to the mass of other men I did and shame on you for the notion. Held you better I did. How you disappoint me.

There are shouts from without, from the harbourside. Mem at labour. With his gaze affixed to the wall and the slipping ripples of firelight thereon Sion tells Catherine that he will take her up to his hovel and make a space in there for her and the children and there they can all remain until he can devise a scheme. Warm and safe up there it is he tells her. It will be pod-tight in there for certain with six heads under one roof but warm and safe it will be and besides there is no other place or option. It will be a brief arrangement only until Sion can build another Ty Nos or put coin by for steerage or some other eventuality. Time and space to think he needs. *When the children awaken,* says Sion. *I will take you all up,* he says.

Down they go into deep time. Time which is kept and reckoned by rock and bored through by hands before them. The lights of lanterns slithering and skittering across the waxy-wet walls of the shaft. Three lanterns one to each man and their shadows lurching and elongated. Deep down into time. A movement back towards an origin and a squalor common to it. Off the rungs they step and stand and narrow is the passage in which they must walk single file and stooped over down the incline to the shaft's end where they have been told the timbers have been tipped and where twisted across the topmost beam and caught in the rocking light of the lead lamp is this tangle of bodies. Mortis-stiffened into postures strange and reaching.

- Ah. Found more than timbers it appears we have boys.

The lamps are lifted to pool illumination.

- Dear God.

Liquid drips.

- Three childer too look. Behold where they have torn the teats for milk.

- Dear Christ.

- The woman says one of the three. - The, the mother. Met her I have. Clearly I do recall for pleasing I found her features. Four, five nights since this was. On a quest to find the vulcan was she.

- The vulcan?

- The new vulcan aye. Sion I believe he is called. From over the mountain he came. As did she. Lives primarily in his forge he does but he keeps a Ty Nos on top in which the widow Richardson does abide with her child.

This twist of grey bodies in the lamplight. The diverse dimensions of them. Generational gradation held stiffly here in mortis deep in this deep burrow. Liquid drips and the three men breathe and their lungs press hard against the rock about them chiselled and riven long ago.

Pulling on a rope the three stand at the entrance to the shaft on the earth's thin scrim. Hand over hand they heave. Feet come out of the shaft braceleted by the cable and blue-black they are with sunken blood and early fester. The flesh abraded at the ankle by the rope and mushed curd-like and spongiform away to bear the bone. Maggots abound. Such a grotesque birth as this is.

In the false dawn they come for him. Kick him awake in his forge and tie him about at the wrists and take him out like that into a prison-cart and blunder him into the mounted cage and chain it secure. Take their seats and slap the horses and their ears are totally deaf to his hollering. They remove him from the port and take him up into the higher lands on the drover's road to Trallwng on which they stop at a pool to water the steeds and their prisoner and relieve themselves too and at the unlocking of the cage Sion leaps kicking and spins off the bank and into the lake and there is the violent shock of immersion and then a momentary calm in which weeds shimmy in a gorgeous green light and then he is hauled back into air again. His bellowing mouth stoppered with a fist.

The men in their dark livery drag the thrashing Sion out of the tarn and lay him flat on its banks. On his back he kicks and screams and spews water like a fabled merman landed. In an element seemingly offensive to his nature. The men yell at him of murder. Foul and pre-meditated. Children. Three children they say. A coven of meat-birds in a tree nearby cackle at the frenzy. A long slow death is what they say. Underground. If not dead from the fall then from starvation. Murder. Beast. Monster. Inhuman. The birds hunch their shoulders and blackly laugh at it all from up in the limbs of the leafless tree.

What is tarn-water and what is the more common wet of snot and tears and piss is impossible to distinguish on Sion's face and clothing and under the chair he is belted to so drenched in it all is he. Here in the back room of a Trallwng tavern. Green decals of chickweed on his face and in his hair and on his ratty clothes and surrounded by men is he. Unsmiling men with faces that in parts have never been touched by a sunbeam.

Sion's body buckled by each sob, the secured and scrawny and bedraggled frame of it. A uniformed man slaps his face again.

- There was a fog Sion is saying. - A thick fog there was. Left them on the ridge nearby to my Ty Nos I did and alive they were when I saw them last. All truth this is. All truth. On top of the surface they were when I left them.

Again he is struck across the face. The crack of the impact off the stone walls loud and not the tiniest flinch from the watching men not at the blow nor at the tooth that skids down Sion's trembling chin.

- You pushed her. You pushed *them*. Childer and all. Motive you had. Black-hearted cunt of a man you rid yourself of their burden. We know what you did. Admit it now and mark a favour with your maker whom you are surely shortly to face.

A sob so big it seems Sion's small body will snap. - I did not push her. I did not push them. I am so sorry.

To the gibbet he is condemned. And prior to that to incarceration in Trallwng gaol where he is to construct his own cage given his storied aptitude for metalwork. And the sounds of this terrible labour from his cell do not cease neither through daylight nor darkness the whack of metal on metal sounds throughout. Never ceases until the day he requests more iron which request is refused and it is decreed that the moment of his doom has come and prognostication is to halt with immediate effect and carried out his sentence will be. Now. Forthwith and with all despatch. No more deferment. The time has arrived.

There is a crossroads at Pen y Crogbren as is meet for the murderers of self and others and that is where he is taken. To the trunk that has been driven into the earth and upon which he is in his gibbet-cage hoisted and hung and left like that. His cage: crested it is with a winged angel in metal with head bowed and hands clasped across the chest. Unique adornment for a gibbet and the dexterity of its design is remarked upon by those who trudge up from the port and other settlements to pelt the criminal with white stones as has long been their custom or other missiles or to spear his skin with sharpened sticks twice the length of a man. Necessary entertainment is this torment and it continues until the miscreant is too weak to wail and thus spoil the fun of it all and there he hangs in the salt-stinging wind up from the sea with the steel bands crushing his body and the smaller rings around his neck and head squeezing ever tighter only to be marginally loosened by emaciation and the flesh that wastes. Known to Sion to the atom is the material of his prison. Up there he reduces as the days go by: shrinks and shrivels and devours himself. For several nights the woman and child in the nearest hovel hear him screaming of *bwyd* and *seren* and *suckling pigs* and *wolves* and of little ones long gone and of a twpsin called Poor Huw. Do not listen, says the woman to her child as they hunker at the hearth and the weather moans and rattles without. She sings to her daughter to fill her ears even through most of the night because the frantic chunner from the crossroads does not stop. *All of us in this ending* are some words she discerns. *You are all I in what will be your end. Look upon me.* Words like that inside the gale. Slowly the sound ceases to be of formed and recognisable words and turns into a raw keening and after that just a gibberish chain of no more meaning than the sound of water over stones and then it stops completely except for two whoops one quickly after the other when a meat-bird takes Sion's eyes. The salt wind has preservative properties yet some scraps do fall away from him and out of him and are snuffled up by scavengers of diverse sorts including one still and moonlit night a furtive and slat-sided bitch wolf that seems of a substance with the very blackness it appears from and returns to after one eye-blink out of it. Time enough just to claim a piece of the gibbet's clasped and collapsing thing.

The skin of Sion becomes a leathery scrim across skull and ribcage in the brined blowings. Waters flow and claim. Great holes are gouged in the earth like the bootprints of new gods titanic and fixated. Gods that stamp. Pits made by massive heels that crush and grind men into the earth as the men themselves crush emmetts. The mountains are moved. Some of them. The lakes too. The sea is scored by the wakes of ships and things spin. The thing in the gibbet outlasts many changes and undergoes such things itself but eventually it must crumble and disassemble into a jumble of tatty bones in the bottom of the cage which will only re-touch the earth when the gibbet-stake itself has fallen in rot long before human skin has been utterly erased. Long before that.

ACKNOWLEDGEMENTS

Mark Schmitt, for too many things to list.

Tom Pickard; the influence abides.

Bill Parry and Frances. Tom, Lester, and Patty Lou Parry.

Mirko Bozic.

Wendy Whidden and Dave (we'll always have The Slaughtered Lamb).

Tariq. Cheers pal.

To Gideon Koppel, for introducing me to Sion y Gof in the first place.

REPEATER BOOKS

is dedicated to the creation of a new reality. The landscape of twenty-first-century arts and letters is faded and inert, riven by fashionable cynicism, egotistical self-reference and a nostalgia for the recent past. Repeater intends to add its voice to those movements that wish to enter history and assert control over its currents, gathering together scattered and isolated voices with those who have already called for an escape from Capitalist Realism. Our desire is to publish in every sphere and genre, combining vigorous dissent and a pragmatic willingness to succeed where messianic abstraction and quiescent co-option have stalled: abstention is not an option: we are alive and we don't agree.